Paddle Back Out

Lucky Streaks and Wipeouts
in The Surf, The Party Circuit and The Legal System

Often dizzy from alcohol oblivion, a Florida waterman and lucky-star criminal lawyer navigates client and personal courtroom battles.

A Novel

By Scott L. Richardson
With Ghostwriter Casey Tennyson

INSIDE:
The lore of The Sunshine State, the surf culture, the party circuit and the legal system set the backdrop for a compelling novel. The lure of substance abuse and adrenaline-filled adventure result in alternating lucky streaks and spills, some with serious legal issues. With a litigator's precision and a story-teller's spin, Author Scott L. Richardson writes in gritty detail about the main character Jack Wander's precarious life from the 1970s for a half century that vacillates between navigating calm glassy sets of waves and calamity-filled events and serious missteps. Not just in surfing, but in many hellraising, harrowing or heartbreaking situations, Jack crashes, overcomes it, shrugs it off, and paddles back out.
Jack gets back.

ABOUT THE AUTHOR:
Scott Richardson practices law throughout the state of Florida from his main office in downtown Orlando. He received a bachelor's degree and a Juris Doctor degree from University of Florida. He lives in Longwood and New Smyrna Beach, Florida.
Learn more about the lawyer and author on www.paddlebackout.com .

ABOUT THIS BOOK

Title
Paddle Back Out

in The Surf, The Party Circuit and The Legal System

Often dizzy from alcohol oblivion, a Florida waterman and lucky-star criminal lawyer navigates client and personal courtroom battles.

A Novel

Published in the USA by
Cutting Edge Communications, Inc.

Written by
Scott L. Richardson

With Ghostwriter
Casey Tennyson

International Standard Book Number
ISBN number 978-0-9855264-5-0

PREFACE BY THE AUTHOR

Over the years, surfing friends ask me about my law practice and legal stories. Lawyer friends ask for surfing and adventure stories. Everyone else seems to ask for both. An inordinate amount of people urged me to write a book.

My life has been surrounded by captivating characters and uncanny extreme circumstances. My niche obsessions of high impact criminal defense trial lawyering, and surfing in both Florida and global surf spots, plunged me into extreme situations. The experiences were often complicated by and compounded by an addictive nature, especially with a hardcore substance abuse history. By virtue of these obsessions and addictions, I was exposed to intimate details of colorful people and scintillating situations. From these experiences, I crafted this fictional account of the main character Jack Wander and other characters with some embroidering and embellishing.

Potential clients, of both mine and other lawyers, can get insights into the legal system. Readers can journey with Jack Wander through a detox in a local jail, a stint at a federal prison and a myriad of legal cases.

The purpose is also to encourage a can-do attitude especially when facing fear and challenges. Advice I give my law firm clients daily is to hang firm to positive thinking. Like in surfing, dust off the last mishap, face the oncoming sets, and paddle back out.

DEDICATION

To Linda, Jesse, Maraya
and to the friends who will smile when they read this book.

CONTENTS

CHAPTERS		PAGE
1	BLACK MARKS ON THE LEGAL SYSTEM	1
2	THE PARRAMORE PARADIGM	6
3	CULTURE AND COURTROOM COMBAT	10
4	WHERE I DWELL TO SELL	14
5	NEW SMYRNA BEACH SUNDAY FUNDAY	17
6	A WINK AND A NOD TO LADY JUSTICE	21
7	ST. THOMAS TO STUDY AND SURF	28
8	MID-1980s AND 8 BALLS IN U.S. VIRGIN ISLANDS	34
9	SALES JOB NOT ON THE RESUME	42
10	OMENS OF FUTURE ALCOHOLISM	45
11	FROM OHIO TO A FLORIDA "HIGH" SCHOOL	49
12.	TRADED MIDWEST FOR FLORIDA'S WILD WEST	52
13.	THE SURFING SWITCH TURNED ON	55
14	SURF LESSONS FROM A SURF SNOB	57
15	THE MINNOW SURFS MAFIA HOUSE	61
16	COIN-TOSS COLLEGE	65
17	GRAD WEEK IN NEW SMYRNA BEACH	66
18	THE ACADEMICS OF UF LIFE	68
19	SATURDAYS SURFING OR ON THE FIELD OF SCREAMS	71
20	THE LAW SCHOOL LIGHTBULB	75
21	THE LAW OF ATTRACTION	78
22	OMENS OF CRIMINAL DEFENSE	85
23	THE BARON HALF IN THE BAG	90
24	A FIRST VICTORY FOR TRUTH, UN MOMENTO DE VERDAD	92
25	TAHITIAN TALE	97
26	BUSTED	101
27	BUSTED NOT BROKEN	105
28	WAIT, GAVEL, WAIT, TRAVEL	107
29	PRISON	108
30	LIMBO TO LITIGATION	117
31	GETTING HIGH AND GETTING BY	120
32	SHATTERED SHELLS TO DETOX HELL	123

33 DOUBLE LIFE TROUBLE 129
34 MAKE IT A DOUBLE 132
35 FOR THE PEOPLE 138
36 THE ABCs OF DEFERRING DETOX 140
37 ALOHA TO DRINKING 142
38 FROM A TO ME 144
39 THE GRIP OF SOBRIETY 146
40 A FLASHLIGHT ON THE LEGAL SYSTEM 148
41 TRYING TO SKIRT THE LAW 156
42 IN PLAIN SIGHT 159
43 MEMORIES AT THE MUSEUM 162

CHAPTER 1, BLACK MARKS ON THE LEGAL SYSTEM

"I'm going to arrest your black ass every time I see you on the street," threatened the cop according to my client Vernon.

"But Officer Winston, I didn't do anything," said Vernon.

"Shut up. Put your hands behind your back," said Officer Winston, as he roughly clamped the handcuffs on the thin wrists of the five-foot-two-inch detainee.

He stuffed the handcuffed Vernon into the sweltering backseat of a Ford patrol car, making sure to smack Vernon's head against the side of the sedan as he shoved him inside.

By policy, procedure and law, this encounter should have been captured in real time on Officer Winston's body camera. It was not. Per usual, Officer Winston decided he wanted to administer a little street justice. His body cam device mystically became inoperable. The temperature reached 98 degrees and 98% humidity. The midday sun magnified the heat inside the unairconditioned car. Winston left Vernon to boil in the backseat while he tore up Vernon's parked vehicle in search of drugs.

The reason for the search was the alleged smell of marijuana. On the arrest affidavit, the officer swore he could smell what he knew to be marijuana through his extensive training and experience. This phantom pot odor had become the easy whimsical excuse for cops to search people's vehicles and homes, in order to secure evidence of alleged wrongdoing. Rogue Florida cops would invoke the magic words, "I smell cannabis," then search as they wished. This overused arbitrary search tactic did not pass the smell test for this lawyer when it came to the legal rights of American citizens. Regardless of my stance on the matter, the sniff and snoop method worked for cops in many cases. From my vantage point, judges in The Sunshine State often believed the version of events as told by a cop regardless of challenges presented to the search by defense attorneys. Uniforms equaled credibility in courtrooms.

In this instance, the officer ransacked Vernon's 2007 Nissan Maxima. He ransacked the seats and the glove compartment, then ripped off the interior door panels leaving the car disheveled and in disarray. For all of his intense efforts, the officer found some white dust and pebbles on the driver's side floor board. He dutifully tested the white powder with an on-scene drug testing kit, widely known in legal circles for being inaccurate. The test allegedly came up positive for cocaine. As a result, Vernon was transported in the police car to the Orange County jail and processed for possession of a controlled substance. Oddly, the reason for the search was pot and none was discovered, so the officer conveniently switched his focus to cocaine. It was another fill-in-the-blank move for this cop in his arrest of this personally targeted citizen.

I got the call at my law office from Vernon. I entered my notice of appearance with the court which notified the prosecutors and court system that I was the attorney of record for Vernon. I demanded discovery, or evidence, with the boiler plate standard form used by criminal defense attorneys. Vernon had assured me, hand-to-God, that there was no dope in his vehicle and the cop was lying when he said he smelled weed. I believed him.

This bullshit went down all the time and drug cases were brought against innocent people who found my office for representation. The alleged illegal substance in one recent case was drywall powder, and in another case the substance was Dunkin' Donuts sugar glaze. In both cases, the cops either miscalculated or misunderstood the on-site drug testing equipment, or they intentionally arrested innocent men. These seemingly ridiculous sources of evidence were all too common.

My client was on the right side of the law. Within three weeks, the assigned prosecutor filed with the court a "no information" notice. Translated, that meant the case was not suitable for prosecution. The white powder was a mixture of sand and small pebbles. My theory was that the cop told a white lie about the white powder and a black man. He knew the evidence was not valid when he arrested Vernon. He did not care. He was making good on his promise to arrest Vernon's black ass whenever he saw him on the street. He knew Vernon would sit in jail for at least a little while and his life would be cruelly disrupted. At a minimum he would have to scratch together a good sum of money to pay a lawyer to defend him on the baseless charges. The officer's spiteful mission was accomplished. I was hired again. I told him, "You raise the cash and I'll raise the doubt." In our system, people accused of crimes are innocent until proven guilty beyond a reasonable doubt in a court of law. I raised the doubt. I got him out of trouble again.

Shortly after that arrest, the vindictive officer spotted Vernon in his car at The Chill Lounge in an Orlando neighborhood occupied almost exclusively by black Americans. The officer was on bicycle patrol this time. He claimed in his arrest report that he saw Vernon pull into a parking space without his seatbelt fastened. He rode up on his bike and screamed at Vernon, "Put all of your windows down now and get out of the car."

Vernon made the grave error of responding, "What did I do Officer Winston?"

Wrong answer! The cop dismounted his bicycle and grabbed Vernon who was snugly seat-belted in the vehicle while parked. The officer violently removed the suspect from the vehicle and pinned him to the ground, handcuffed him, and stuffed him into a different officer's patrol vehicle. Again, with maniacal focus, he ripped Vernon's car apart in search of anything illegal. He came up empty again. The officer now was being recorded on cell phones of people standing around the scene so he had no chance to dummy-up evidence. Vernon took the ride anyway to the County jail this time for resisting arrest without violence. Again, a seemingly baseless charge but one that the state attorney would stick to and prosecute to the end, probably just because they had seen Vernon's name too many times in the system.

The prosecutors took the case to trial. The jury took about 15 minutes to come back with a not guilty verdict. That was alright with the ruthless officer though, because Vernon had been greatly inconvenienced and had to pay his attorney, me, a handsome fee for a jury trial.

I spoke with the jurors after the proceedings. They did not believe a word the police officer had said. They could not understand how a man could be arrested for resisting arrest without violence when they could not see a reason for the arrest from the start.

When I was conducting voir dire, which means jury selection, I had posed the question to the jurors as to whether or not they kept up with local news. I committed to memory those who answered in the affirmative. The reason was that there had been a number of local TV news stories immediately prior to Vernon's trial about police misconduct and wrongful convictions. The literal translation of voir dire is "to speak the truth." In this moment, I wanted the jurors on Vernon's case to be truthful in their decision about his case through listening to the evidence. Thankfully, they did choose truth.

I have learned that a trial may be won or lost on jury selection. Jury selection is a creative art form like writing or creating music. Seating this jury was dicey, like snow skiing over moguls on double black diamond runs. Like in any case, there was no blueprint, but rather unique real-time decision making for each trial. From the very beginning, when the potential jurors, filed into the room, I started sizing them up to gauge if they were liberal minded or fair. I am often wrong about the first impression. Then the questions started from the judge about basic information of the jury panel such as marital status, occupation, and prior juror experience. The prosecutor then asked questions from a script given from their supervisors. Then it was the defense attorney's turn. Even though it was not necessarily advisable, I gave subliminal clues to start predisposing jurors to my way of thinking through creative questioning. I discerned who might be sympathetic to my client or the case. On this day, there were 18 potential jurors for a misdemeanor. The defense got to strike three for no reason, the prosecutor got to strike three, then there were strikes for causes, to weed out would-be jurors. Then the judge, prosecutor and defense attorney started with the first juror and proceeded one-by-one to seat a jury of six plus one alternate. More serious crimes have more jurors but it follows the same protocols.

Just because a trial is scheduled on a certain day does not mean the client actually gets to see a judge that day. Sometimes you arrive at court and multiple trials are set for the same day. The judge decides which trials will go that day and in what order. Sometimes they are postponed. If your case is up then the court orders a jury panel. Criminal defense lawyering is nerve-wracking with a lot of hurry up and wait. The clients are already rattled that their life is on the line and the unpredictable nature of the process unnerves them even more. It is my job to communicate well and keep them at ease the best that I can by reassuring them. You get used to the wild-and-wooley nature of the waiting game.

With a few normal schedule changes, we got Vernon in and out of this trial. Apparently, our jury selection was effective, along with a valid legal defense, as evidenced by the quick not guilty verdict.

Not long after this trial, Vernon was attempting to leave The Chill Lounge at 2 a.m. on another sultry humid night. Tensions had gotten really ugly between this cop and this citizen. Again, as the encounter began, the officer made sure not to engage his body cam. Again, on a bicycle, the officer allegedly screamed at Vernon to stop his car for another nonexistent seat belt issue. Now fearing desperately for his physical safety, his liberty, and his dignity, Vernon continued to wheel slowly out of The Chill Lounge. The officer took great exception as Vernon tried to ease out of the parking lot around parked cars, so he pulled out his ASP baton, a device to target large muscle groups of humans, and smashed the driver side window of Vernon's car. Vernon slowly left the parking lot and the irate officer, in an effort to peacefully go home. Meanwhile, the officer was radioing Orlando Police Department fellow cops that he had a suspect fleeing in attempt to elude arrest. He added that the suspect tried to run him over so the suspect would be charged with aggravated assault on a police officer. Rightfully so, nothing gets police attention more than reported violence against another policeman. Four cars converged on and stopped Vernon who complied. They jerked him out of his vehicle, handcuffed him and arrested him again, this time for something that could give him real prison time. While the officer had yet again failed to activate his body cam per law and procedure, the other officers had not failed in that obligation. The bullying was documented. They nicknamed him Flamingo because he was wearing a flashy shirt. They taunted him about their idea that he didn't have a real job. The footage of Vernon being stopped, harassed and arrested was hard for me to watch.

CHAPTER 2, THE PARAMORE PARADIGM

The ridiculing arresting cops were actually correct about my client Vernon's flimsy employment status. The jobless and underemployed lifestyle patterns of Vernon and his neighbors were deep-seated. Vernon was born and raised in the Paramore District of Orlando, just west of downtown, where about a quarter of the residents are typically unemployed. The historic African American neighborhood experienced poverty and desperate conditions since slavery in the 1800s to modern day. Vernon grew up in Paramore with little money, few positive role models, and a nonchalant vision for the future. Like many of his neighbors, he was unemployed, uneducated and burdened with a serious criminal record. Residents like Vernon found very few ways out of the crime-filled area. If they could get a job, it would be low-paying. With their lack of income or low income, they surely would be stuck in the neighborhood. They could sell drugs; that was always a tempting option for better financial standing in the neighborhood.

I drove through Paramore recently investigating a case and the plight of the residents clicked in one 360-degree image at a stop light. Within sight of Camping World Stadium, where the lucky few might escape Paramore and perform as star athletes, the vibe was grim. A filthy man teetered on a trash can perch, whiling away his day asleep gripping a bulky brown paper bag. A faded Martin Luther King mural peeled on a wall behind warehouses with barbed wire fencing. Rotting picket fences, rusting chain link fences and a weathered wrought iron gate failed at keeping out the crime from the humble aging cinder block dwellings painted in a mix of muted pastels. Under roofs missing shingles, moldy walls with chipping stucco had metal black bars on windows which hinted at further futile attempts to keep crime outside of the homes. The neighborhood was still in the morning with little foot traffic. Typically, dusk marks party time for those living off the government dole. It was mid-month so there was no line at the convenience store with the handwritten "checks cashed here" sign. When I've been in Paramore on the first of the month when the welfare checks arrive from the government, I've seen the neighbors stand in long lines waiting to cash their government-issued meager allotments.

The public park sat eerily vacant. Logically if residents weren't working, it would seem they might be with their children. On this day, they were not. There were no children. There were no lights on in the dismal dwellings. The most telling neighbor on the streets that morning was a young man riding a bicycle ignoring his puppy companion. The pup with no leash dutifully ran close to the bike's back tire as it navigated through the four-way vehicle traffic. My Golden Retriever with no restraint would run right out into the cars. Most pet owners would be afraid their dog would get hurt. In Paramore, it's survival of the fittest. The ones that survive get real smart about cars, and danger of all kinds, as a pure natural selection for survival. Just like the puppy following with no physical ties to the biker, the Paramore residents tend to stay stuck in their cycles for generation after generation.

The Paramore population with these difficult conditions have numerous encounters with police because, even if they were not committing crimes, their neighbors were. Vernon, at age 48, had taken measures to clean up his life. Despite his best efforts, his past, his neighborhood, and his ongoing clash with Officer Winston, were keeping him down in life.

For one Paramore neighbor, I decided enough is enough. This cop clearly had a twisted dynamic and attitude towards Vernon. In due course, I filed my notice of appearance as attorney for Vernon and started investigating the facts of the latest arrest. This time I demanded Brady Material which is deemed exculpatory; meaning evidence favorable to the defendant or may be damaging to one of the prosecutions' witnesses. What was revealed was not entirely a surprise but horrifying nonetheless. The gist was that this officer had already been reprimanded for failing to use his body cam properly. The most disturbing event was while he gave chase to another suspect with his body cam was turned off, which was not authorized by Orlando Police Department or OPD policy, and the suspect came up bloody and beaten.

In addition to Brady Material, I made a public records request demanding all Internal Affairs reports on this officer and any subsequent discipline. Sure enough, when the information was delivered to my office, Officer Winston had been reprimanded by OPD for failing to activate his body cam when he encountered suspects, which was in direct violation of police procedure. The officer had a history of doing so at the critical moments of encounters between himself and black civilians.

I previously beat back several weak cases that had been charged against

Vernon. The state attorney did not help him through his litany of troubles. I found the whole ordeal frustrating.

I interacted and communicated with cops every day as it related to my cases and my clients. I simply wanted them and expected them to tell the truth. Instead they seemed to waffle and waiver and continue their attacks on minorities just playing pool, smoking weed and not bothering anyone. The brotherhood of cops did not like this mamsy-pamsy attorney questioning their mighty authority and digging into their backgrounds. They did not like that I asked that they follow the law and use their body cams. A number of cops that patrolled Paramore referred to themselves as proactive patrol. They rode on bikes and were street level to blend in and become friendly with citizens, but it had the opposite effect. Respect had to be earned and had to go both ways. The divide was disturbing to see on video after video of Vernon's unwarranted arrests for the times when the cops actually did activate their body cams.

Around the same time as Vernon's multiple arrests, Officer Winston received praise by the Chief of Police because he made so many arrests. In my opinion, his arrests were not deserving of accolades, as they appeared racially motivated, and often based on fabrications. The misused power divided the country when the cops operated on the concept of "Might Makes Right."

While the case was pending against Vernon for the aggravated assault on a police officer, I received a call from Vernon. He said to turn on the TV news, that Officer Winston was being publicly reprimanded for misuse of his body cam. I caught the end of the news segment then looked it up online on the TV station website. The news reported that two officers turned off their body cams after an illegal pursuit and once again a suspect was injured. Ironically, Officer Winston was being disciplined on the news by the same Chief of Police that previously commended him.

Just like everyday citizens are accountable for following our laws, our police should follow our laws as well. Jack Wander is not a cop-hater. From what I see, the vast majority of cops carry out their duties with integrity. I believe law enforcement officers should earn much more than they are currently paid for putting their lives on the line each day. Their job cannot be easy. They also should undergo in-depth psychological evaluations before they take the job, and get extensive training on crowd control and violence de-escalation methods. Without effective law enforcement, our country could not peacefully exist. The police are a valued part of our community. The bad apples sour the reputation of the police forces, in much the same way as greedy, dishonest or lazy lawyers diminish the reputation of the legal community.

CHAPTER 3, CULTURE AND COURTROOM COMBAT

When people hear the name Jack Wander uttered in my jurisdiction, some smile, some shake their heads and some cringe. The thought bubbles above their heads say, "Wow, Jack's a force in the courtroom," or "Man, Jack is one lucky dude," or "Oh my gosh, Jack is a nutcase." In fairness to the divided perceptions, I have earned all of these labels. For over 30 years I have been a street lawyer defending America's citizens. I have had a colorful career including some well publicized missteps.

I am not in the profession just for the money, although the rate of pay makes for a gratifying lifestyle. I have high end clients that pay their whole fee up front. They make my year in terms of income. One affluent lady accidentally took a handgun through airport security and got arrested at Orlando International Airport en route to sell her estate in France. Another well-to-do lady got into an emotional altercation with a stranger and grabbed her arm and she faced a battery charge. An internationally renowned physician and entrepreneur was accused of taking up-the-skirt videos of ladies in public without their knowledge. Professional athletes find themselves in my office with legal skirmishes, too. High profile and high roller clients don't hesitate to stroke six figure checks to get out of their legal trouble.

I have some middle-of-the-road clients, who can't pay top dollar, but they can pay reasonable fees.

Then I have those clients that can't afford my services at those rates but they manage to pay something. In my mind, if I'm not going after it every day, thereby establishing my presence with the judges and the other lawyers, then I'd lose my edge. I enjoy what I do. It's sport to me. I don't turn away clients if they don't have money in their pockets to pay me at that time. I don't have a set rate. I take cases that earn a range of rates, because I feel the need to practice and know who all the players are in my legal community at all times.

Managing and navigating this wide range of clients through the system when they are confronted with allegations against them by the government is wildly complicated. Each criminal defendant comes with different expectations as to what fate they face based on charges levied against them. If they are first time offenders, they can require astounding amount of time for hand-holding. Some want specifics as to what to wear, even how to wear their hair, logistics to get to the courthouse, who to bring with them and so forth. This requires a personal touch from the attorney. To give proper personal client service, I instruct my clients on all of the above, plus the legal advice.

Not only attire, but courtroom decorum is critical. Make no mistake that the defendant is being watched closely by everyone in the room. Some of the less sophisticated clients tend to act out in the courtroom when they feel witnesses are lying against them or things are not going their way for some other reason.

Let's take Vernon for example. I was once again arguing for Vernon, the cop-bullied black man, in a high conflict motion. I was staring at the judge from the podium fielding his complicated, precise legal questions and so was the prosecutor. The judge was so bright that I had to focus intently on his compound questions to give him succinct, on-point answers. Halfway through one of the judge's long-winded inquiries, he gazed past me and he held up his hand to stop the proceedings.

He directed his communication to Vernon sitting behind me where I could not see him, "Sir, do not make facial expressions and do not shake your head. Please do not stare down the state attorney or witnesses. Keep your gestures to yourself. You are not helping your case. Mr. Wander will talk to you about your courtroom behavior."

I asked appalled, "Is that what he's doing behind me?"

I looked around and Vernon was flashing his grill of gold teeth all around. He looks like the actor Samuel Jackson in a smaller frame. He was dressed to the nines in 1970s powder blue bellbottom pants and a vest, a white shirt with a wide collar and frilly sleeves and blue fake alligator suede shoes. Before court dates, my office sends a letter instructing clients to dress as though they are going to church. Vernon went to a thrift shop and suited himself for a retro disco instead. He just doesn't understand life outside of Parramore.

I was mortified and pissed off in a big way. My sleepless nights, my research, my hard labor, and my laying it on the line in front of my professional peers ... and this jackass can't behave in court. No doubt, after court he would be one of the clients not grateful for my services either.

In court, he watched me argue with the judge and prosecutor. We had a lot of highbrow legalese terms flying back and forth. I live for this sort of jousting over complicated cases. The intelligent judge used the Socratic method to ask questions to resolve the conflict.

While I was making headway like a son-of-a-bitch and heading toward the end zone legally speaking, the client was lost in space. In Vernon's case, like many others, we walk out of the courtroom after 90 minutes of combat and he looks at me and asks, "What just happened?"

Exasperated, I answer, "We're winning Vernon, we're winning."

Instead of being appreciative, he looked at me incredulously and demanded, "This isn't winning. This is bullshit. I'm innocent, man! Why the hell can't you get this thrown out like you did before? What's wrong?"

I responded, "I believe you but I have to convince the people in the courtroom that you are right. You are working against yourself by acting like a fool in the courtroom to the point where the judge tells me to take you outside and give you a lecture, so keep your grill closed and shut up."

This is the lack of gratitude a lawyer sometimes gets for years of education and thousands of hours on the legal battlefields. Vernon paid a sizeable fee based on his income, and he certainly got his bang for his buck for legal services. The mentality of some clients such as Vernon is just "give me, give me." Even if I give a break on fees, or give extra time or attention, some still want more from me.

As we got in the courtroom elevator to leave, Vernon was finished with the courtroom drama and already off to the next series of crisis in his life, "I've got to get my phone back, man. I ain't got no money. My girl said she had my baby, but I think it's another dude's. She ain't my baby mama."

As pissed as I was at him, I had to remember he's not bad-people. Vernon comes from a way different culture than I. He's a Paramore guy. He's street. This stereotype is what laymen picture mentally when I say I am a defense attorney. It is, in fact, part of my client base. I don't give up on these guys. Hope springs eternal that I positively impact one person, one family, one neighborhood, one community, with ripples through society. Everyone deserves a chance even if they continue to sabotage their chances, even Vernon. I've been given a bucketful of second chances so I understand people need to restart sometimes more than once.

This case with the black mark on the law enforcement and legal community didn't make it to the stage of public awareness that I had anticipated. It ended with a pop gun and not a nuclear explosion. I planned to make a big PR splash out of the continual mistreatment of this man by a vengeful cop. I had expected to make a big mark on the local legal system defending Vernon in court, and possibly even get media coverage. Instead, the case quietly vanished. The day before the case was eventually called for trial, yet another new prosecutor was named and The State dismissed all charges. The prosecutors change often on the cases, as the revolving door of newbie lawyers cycle through the legal system learning curve.

While the Vernon case didn't bring media coverage as I had anticipated, or prestige in the legal community, the system itself knows what happened. The courtroom walls have ears. Judges talk. The various clerical staffs talk. They know when you are a force. That's how criminal defense attorney reputations are really made and disseminated. Like the wind, it just is. Young attorneys ask where I get my cases, well, it's not from television advertising, mainstream media or a buzzy website. If you tap into the word on the street for criminal defense representation, you will likely call Jack Wander.

CHAPTER 4, WHERE I DWELL TO SELL

Unlike my client Vernon, I've had a semi-charmed life. The phrase was used in lyrics by the band Third Eye Blind. I achieved semi-charmed instead of charmed status I suppose from my plethora of unorthodox choices. I've had lucky breaks and peaks in success dinged with numerous self-implosions.

Young lawyers ask how I get so many clients. Here's the deal: there are currently 300 lawyers who will take a criminal case in Orlando. Challenges for me in attracting new clients can be that my resume, bio, Florida Bar history and rap sheet tell a story of a less than perfect lawyer. Counter intuitively, my past has the kind of blemishes and scars that make a lawyer one of the very best choices to defend someone.

The State Bar has scrutinized me on many occasions, none of which had to do with the actual law firm or my performance as an attorney. I've never touched funds in escrow which did not belong to me. Some lawyers succumb to the temptation to dip into client funds held in their control. I've never misappropriated clients' funds or committed malpractice. I've been nothing but a committed advocate for the downtrodden and both the rightly and wrongly accused. My ethics, competency and my courtroom presence has never come into question. I am one of those A-listers of the legal community. I am an A-lister with a B. The B stands for blemishes.

While my actual law practice has been sterling for north of 30 years, my personal life has not. Decades ago, cocaine-fueled escapades, misadventures and subsequent arrests caused a multiple year loss of my privilege to practice law and cost me time in a federal prison. Having overcome those blemishes, I was only to lose the privilege a second time when the demon alcohol took my life over and again I engaged in ill-advised behavior on a personal level which caught The Bar's attention. Arrests for DUIs and disorderly conduct and the like didn't fare well for my legal career. My trouble was public. The Florida Bar News, the industry publication for lawyers and judges, reports every issue on lawyers being disciplined, suspended and disbarred. I got ink several times.

The first time I stopped practicing law, Jack Wander got popped so people wrote me off saying, "Bye-bye asshole."

Then I hung my new office sign a few years later. Clients came in, one after the other.

Why? Because my first time in trouble with my time in prison, people liked me and their families liked me. It seems so incongruent and inconsistent but it was a fantastic place to meet potential clients.

Then a few years later, I drank myself into oblivion, and agreed to make my law license inactive, and I bounced back a second time. I got a firehose of clients from going to rehab centers, AA meetings and recovery group meetings.

By having a hard-knock life, coupled with being a competent attorney, success was my fate. I've been in so much trouble: Arrested? Check. Felony conviction? Check. Jail time? Check. Prison time? Check. More than 10 times in drug and alcohol rehab? Check. Smuggled drugs from the Caribbean? Check. Divorced? Well, hell yes, check given the aforementioned checklist.

That's it. That is my secret. It's no secret at all. It's never been a secret because my mishaps were on television news and newspapers for the whole nosey world to see.

I still hear the rumblings. I sense the murmurs. I catch the whispers. I'll see a previous client in the courthouse with another attorney and ask why he didn't hire me again and he'll tell me he heard I wasn't practicing. People can be petty. They can try to sabotage my practice but it remains steady and secure. Others ask how I can have so many clients when I lived half of my life on my back drunk. I just get the job done. My clients know this. A defendant gets me 24/7 to talk to them. I don't practice theoretical law. I've been in their shoes. I've been busted, prosecuted and sent to prison. My clients feel the vibe of genuine concern for their case through personal knowledge. That is the secret sauce.

The bottom line is that I have dwelled in many places where self-respecting lawyers don't dare tread. I hung out in circles and in places where lawyers just don't go. My unconventional past, and the people I met along the way, continue to feed the beast of a thriving criminal defense and family law practice.

Wherever they come from, when I sign a new client, in reality they want to know less about me and more about their situation. They ask about my win-loss record and my opinion about the outcome of their case.

Potential clients ask how many wins and losses I have. For a DUI example, I try to get it reduced to reckless driving with community service and DUI school. I would estimate 60% of my cases end in compromise and another 40% in outright dismissals or a negotiated resolution. For example, if a client is charged with a DUI and I plea bargain for no conviction and a lesser charge, is that a victory? Is that a win? For the defense attorney, the answer is yes. Does the client think it's a victory? It depends on the client's perception. Some are appreciative because when they first hired their lawyer they were looking down the barrel of a certain conviction with the attendant probationary period, mandated steep auto insurance rate hikes, cumbersome drug and alcohol counseling sessions, and a legal record that a client has to explain away for the rest of a client's life.

When I first meet with a prospective client I tell them what the worst outcome for facing certain convictions and obligations. I mold the client's expectations up front at a reasonable level. I usually do this with a poker face knowing from experience that I can likely deliver a more favorable outcome. If a client demands a guaranteed dismissal of charges, or sole child custody, or some other ultimatum, I send them packing because my experience is that type of client will never be satisfied.

The child custody matter brings me to the other area of law that I practice, family law. In divorces nobody wins. Winning depends again on perception. Divorce is an unhappy situation regardless of outcomes in the courts.

In my career, I deal with a lot of unhappy people with very real concerns. I am immersed in serious big life issues that impact lives. So, in my downtime, I dwell where I immerse myself in the peaceful waters of the ocean, surfing with my brothers. I get a lot of referrals from my surfing friends, too, but mainly I am with them as my trusted tribe.

CHAPTER 5, NEW SMYRNA BEACH SUNDAY FUNDAY

For dedicated trial lawyers and litigators, the stress, angst, and pressure have to be balanced. In my case, Jack Wander loves the physical and mental serene respite through surfing. During high school, college, law school, and into current day, my life has always been in lock step with the world of surfing and my like-minded comrades. Surfing seems like a very simple act to ride a wave to the beach. In reality, surfing is a fairly complex endeavor that necessitates analyzing a conjunction of forces such as wind, tides, speed and nature. At the same time, surfing is unique in that the mission statement of riding a wave is clear. The unpredictability of surfing is a metaphor for life and all that life throws at us. Life is a wave, Albert Einstein even said so.

I played organized sports over my lifetime which was subject to rules, referees, and regulations. Surfing with my buddies on the other hand, there was no right or wrong. I just paddled back out and got into the session. For a lifetime recreational surfer, for myself and my tribe, the pursuit of surfing is not a trial of skill but instead an expression of great pleasure. The simplicity of the sport requires just three things: a surfer, a surfboard, and a wave.

Amazing front man for Pearl Jam, Eddie Vedder, put it this way, "There's something about surfing ... these waves come from 2,000 miles away sometimes. These swells, they crack in a kind of firework, and you ride the firework and give it meaning, and you're connected to nature. It's like no other thing I've felt except for maybe music. And holding your newborn."

Over my semi-charmed life, I have surfed and partied with the same group of guys since our teen years. In the late 1980s, we still met at the Volusia County Fairgrounds parking lot, off of Interstate 4. Per usual, we argued good-naturedly who would drive from there. The destination was typically New Smyrna Beach, depending upon surf conditions. On this day, Weasel D drove us in The Green Machine, his old Ford Ranger. We finished the trek to New Smyrna and drove from the mainland over the north causeway to the peninsula.

To the south, the public beach ends at Canaveral National Seashore. The undeveloped beach has walking trails with wildlife and bird watching. It's also a known clothing optional beach so we stayed clear of that area. The

13-mile public beach is lined mostly with condo buildings, with a few houses, and a few hotels and restaurants. The beach has about a dozen entrances manned with toll booths to pay for daily or annual passes. We drove down Flagler Avenue past the historic shops and restaurants and entered the beach at the east end.

In New Smyrna visitors can drive on the wide beach. Conservationists hate it. Developers love it. Surfers are mixed with the idea. Nonetheless, the drivable beach provides easy access to the coveted waves of the inlet. The inlet is where the more serious surfers compete for waves. Along the pristine stretch of coastline, the other sandbar breaks offer countless surfing opportunities.

We bantered inside The Green Machine. Surfers tend to talk about the conditions, look at waves, analyze waves, overanalyze waves, and then re-overanalyze waves before making a paddle out decision. On this day, a swell and a breeze were coming in from the east. The waves were in the two to three-foot range, super ridable and user-friendly. We headed left toward Ponce Inlet which is on the very north end that separates New Smyrna Beach from South Daytona Beach. We drove north just two miles and parked at a spot affectionately known to our group as Freak Peak, an enjoyable little surf spot.

Freak Peak is just south of the inlet which has a hive of aggressive and wave-hogging locals and professional surfers. Instead, it is a spot where you can pick off your fair share of waves and have semi-solitude for you and your crew to have an invigorating and enjoyable surf session. The waves are steeper, faster and longer at the actual inlet, but the cost is high when it comes to fighting for your market share of the waves. Antagonistic combative types who paddle into the same waves that you are riding shift a surf session from being calm and relaxing. Speed, motion and fiberglass colliding can mean trips to Bert Fish Medical Center for stitches ... or worse.

People worry about sharks but there are more injuries from surf accidents than shark bites, although, New Smyrna is the shark bite capital of the world according to SURFER magazine. That notion might be scary to most, but these little sharks just nip at you. If a shark bites a surfer in California, Hawaii, or Pacific locales, there's a better chance sharks will kill surfers simply because the predators are bigger in the Pacific. Volusia County surfers find the smaller Florida versions more of a nuisance, however, the sharks make for good war stories when trying to pick up beach girls after surfing.

This spring day when I was a young lawyer, we paddled out at Freak Peak at dawn and surfed till mid-afternoon. Afterwards, we hit JB's Fish Camp at the south end of the peninsula on A1A. The dive bar was a spartan looking place in a remote location with a limited casual menu and plenty of booze. It had a boat ramp and was one of the few places in New Smyrna where beachgoers could park a truck and boat trailer. In the 1970s and 1980s, the haunt catered to mostly fishermen out of the adjacent Mosquito Lagoon, with occasional surfers and other watermen. Mosquito Lagoon made a name as the redfish capital of the world and host to numerous fishing tournaments. The self-proclaimed accolade "World Famous" was added on JB's printed paper menus as the hole-in-the-wall gained popularity. Over time the rustic refuge transitioned into a hot spot for all sorts of people, such as surfers, beach condo dwellers, tourists, and, for our purposes, single young women.

On this day, we started with pitchers of beer, crabmeat cocktails and chicken wings. As usual, pitchers of beer morphed into shots of whiskey and beer chasers.

I had a serious day in court the following day, so I was trying not to get obliterated. But ... if you are under the persuasion of an alcoholic in training, too much is never enough. I ordered more rounds.

We were buzzed and spotted some hotties. We boasted of tales about the sharks in loud voices so the chicks could hear us. Like magic, the shark bait worked. Our prey was getting hooked. We were getting inviting looks from a table of girls on the deck. Just about the time my buddies and I started to amble over to their table, another group of suitors made the same move at the same time. It was awkward for us dudes standing around like in "The Bachelor" television show vying for female favor. The five attractive tanned young ladies at the picnic table were soaking in all the male attention. They readily struck up a conversation with all of us. While six of us guys were awkwardly standing at the girls' table, the conversation flowed a little easier with a server's delivery of a tray full of shots ranging from lemon drops to mudslides ordered by yours truly.

One of the gals closest to me, a brunette, asks, "So, what do you do for a living?"

I loved that question in flirtatious situations.

Several guys answered, and my friend answered for me adding humor, "I'm an escaped convict and Jack is my lawyer."

A guy from the other group spouted, "Bullshit."

I ignored him and told the brunette where my office was and other minor details.

The naysayer continued, "I have friends who are lawyers and you are not one."

I've always looked young for my age. Since the 1970s, I wore my hair long and generally bleached very blonde from the sun. In my mid-20s, right out of law school, even in a suit and tie, people said I didn't look like a lawyer. Here in baggies and flip flops, I likely didn't.

In an effort to shoot me down in front of the girls, the dude snidely remarked, "So Mr. Attorney, what does res ipsa loquitur mean?"

"How in the world do you know that phrase?" I asked the bowed-up competitor.

"My dad's a lawyer," he sneered.

"Do you mean the way it's used in pleadings or the real meaning?" I snapped back for clarification.

"I'm a literal guy so I'd like the literal translation," he said.

"It means the thing speaks for itself," I responded being extra careful not to slur or sound as buzzed as I was so I would impress the females, or at least get this guy to back off the aggression.

I lucked out because it was one of five Latin terms that I knew. Thank goodness for law school in this encounter. My harasser stood in stunned silence with his tail tucked between his legs. I had the girls' rapt attention about this point and they snickered at what was now the losing team for the female afternoon frolic.

One of my surfing buddies whispered before he settled into the seat next to the blonde, "I can't believe you pulled that out of your ass."

It turns out, the girls were from Orlando. With only an hour drive to the beach, once you turn 16 and get a driver's license, New Smyrna becomes the weekend social scene.

So, this social encounter on this day turned into a real party scene and continued into a long and late night. Sunday morphed into Monday morning which I was trying to avoid. Another wild drinking adventure moved from the beach to my bed.

CHAPTER 6, A WINK AND A NOD TO LADY JUSTICE

I don't use an alarm clock. I sure was alarmed though when I looked at my digital clock and it showed 7:48 a.m. I was due in court downtown at 8:30 a.m. sharp. Actually, I told my client I would be there 15 minutes early to go over critical paperwork.

I peeked through my bloodshot eyes with dark bags under them, and saw pink lacey thongs on the floor with a blue Hawaiian print sundress. I looked to the left and in the bed was a brunette I met the day prior at the beach. I remembered nothing past a round of shots at the picnic table at JB's Fish Camp in New Smyrna Beach on my Sunday Funday post-surf drinking binge. I remembered nothing of the girl coming home with me.

What I did remember was that I was due in court. I got dressed at breakneck speed without waking my new friend, whatever her name was. In a Superman style drastic character change, I had to make a stark transition from bad-boy partier to respectable barrister. I was young and bullet-proof. I had ways to overcome my ills. I had to take a shot of vodka to shave because my hand was shaking so badly. That was the second task to navigate the day. The first task was to shake the negative thoughts that cross my mind waking from a deep, dark place. The 25 minutes it took to get ready, a simple daily list of tasks for most people, seemed hours. It seems rote, but it was a tall order in my condition to wash my hair, pick out clothes, find my keys. I didn't eat anything although I knew I should. Some people believe if you eat food it soaks up the odor of alcohol, but it seemed like a myth to me.

I scrambled into my suit and sprayed on extra cologne because I knew I still reeked of alcohol. Alcoholics and hard drinkers emit an odor of alcohol, and especially next-day odor of alcohol is stale, distinct and gross. Often, I would be talking to people in the course of practicing law, and they would ask, "Do you smell alcohol?" or, "Did you have a martini lunch?" Probably thousands of people smelled my scent and didn't call me out on it. Once I realized I emitted alcohol fumes, I became self-conscious. I got skilled at holding my breath while talking to people then exhaling when I'd get a few steps away. I learned to stay downwind from people. I sat strategically to give distance from other people. I brought a handkerchief to wipe sweat, and breath mints to camouflage my scent. I learned all of these machinations because the smell doesn't go away in four hours of sleep.

While trying to hurry, I predictively hit every red light between Altamonte Springs where I lived at the time and the Orange County Magnolia Avenue courthouse. I had no time to stop by my office to get files for the hearing. At that time, before the wide use of laptop computers and digital files, we had to lug around heavy cardboard boxes of paper documents. On this day, I'm not sure I would have had the strength to carry around the dense bulky boxes. Just getting to the courthouse was a complete cluster. I sipped on a large coffee cup filled with a screwdriver. I had to drink the orange juice and vodka just to maintain my blood alcohol level. I looked to the left and right and other drivers looked like shiny pennies. The sober strangers on Interstate 4 looked so fresh. I envied their simple lives. For me in my toxic state, driving a car was precarious. I was not confident and between the paranoia and lack of coordination, I parked several blocks from the courthouse where there were more spaces so I didn't have to navigate tight parking spots. I was concerned with scraping my car or other vehicles. I clumsily parked my brown Nissan 300ZX sports car with suede interior and T-tops. Back in the day we rode short boards which fit inside our cars. I was too hammered to take it out when I got home from the beach, so my board was still beside me with the coconut scented wax melting. The board smelled fruity and I smelled like a bum. I was starting to sweat the toxins out of my body.

The closer the courthouse got into my field of vision, the more fear set in of negotiating the day with my hangover and toxicity. I started to see acquaintances close to the entrance of the courthouse as unnatural sweat was continuing to pour out of me and my nose was running from the cocaine from the night before. Once I got to the elevator, I felt doomed to be detected. People wanted to be friendly and chatty and I just wanted to hide. To avoid a brouhaha at the bottom of the elevator, I bounded up the grey marble steps keeping a steady hand on the sturdy metal bannisters to the second floor, where I would hope to run into less people. That was quite a feat in the government building for the people and by the people. All those people mingled in the foyer and hallways with suited lawyers bargaining for favors from the legal elite in the robes. It was a different time. The police, the accused, the lawyers, the judges and interested citizens socialized and bantered cases in the courtroom public spaces. I would pinpoint pockets of human void, and size up the free spaces like a soccer player on the field or a surfer in the wave line-up. Then I would dart. I created all of these gymnastics but none were foolproof.

Once I got to the courtroom, I focused on the clerk station. To my great relief, my dear friend, another person of the party ilk, was in control of the courtroom that day. Regardless of what the attorneys or judges do in court that day, the clerk was charged with memorializing everything that takes place in a court session.

I was not to be scorned or chastised for being late because the judge had not made it to the bench yet.

I was there representing my client Jared who was charged for the fifth time with felony counts of cannabis possession. The prosecutor was not playing anymore. After depositions and every possible motion to suppress under the Fourth Amendment, which attempts to have evidence thrown out because law enforcement had violated the tenets of search and seizure laws, this was the last possible legal effort. The goal was to have the State Attorney agree to sanctions so Mr. Jared Jones would not be incarcerated. He had a family to support and he had to keep working. This was a turning point in this man's life.

At this point, I wished I were not hungover and toxic.

The State Attorney, while pleasant, had to represent the State of Florida and recommended a sentence for my client of 364 days in the County jail. His decision was firm. The vast majority of criminal cases ended in plea bargains. It was like buying a car. The seller, or prosecutor, started high. The buyer, or defense lawyer, started low and negotiated touting all the positives about their client such as their job history, their family life, and also how the client may have been overcharged or accused of a harsher crime than actually committed. The prosecutor typically countered with comments of who was aggrieved by the client's conduct and sometimes corrected the defense attorney as to the actual rap sheet of the client. The client often would lie or intentionally forget their criminal history when hiring their attorney. Hard to believe, but this was true.

The final offer was given to my client, who was also hungover, and he balked. I assured him even if the sentence was pronounced that he would not do jail time.

"How?" Jared demanded.

"If you can keep your shit together, you'll have no jail time. If you draw attention to yourself, you will do jail time," I advised sternly.

The judge got on the bench an hour and ten minutes late. He appeared to be hungover, too. I wondered if the whole world was hungover from Sunday Funday.

We filled out our plea forms. The forms advised the client that he was giving up his right to have a jury trial before his peers, the right to testify, the right to remain silent, and he was advised he may be deported from the country if he was not a U.S. citizen.

The client was asked to approach the podium. The plea colloquy, which is the discussion between the judge and the accused, bantered back and forth about my client's future. The judge asked my client if he understood what he was accused of and if he understood his rights that he was waiving by making a no contest or guilty plea. After the hearing, with input and arguments for the defense and State Attorney, there was little option but to sentence my client to 364 days in the Orange County jail. He was sentenced for a year minus the one day he served when he was arrested.

After sentencing, I shot my friend the clerk "The Look." She returned "The Look" with "The Wink." This eye contact communication solidified the outcome for my client and also committed me to cocktails and party favors for Erin.

I walked back to the jail holding area with my client who purportedly had just been sentenced to a year in jail.

"Don't say a damn word. You'll be out today," I advised curtly at a cautiously chosen moment where we had privacy.

"What's going on?" my scared client asked.

"You'll be out today. Just keep your mouth shut," I affirmed.

The clerk wrote the sentence. The clerk was on the party circuit. The clerk liked to drink and snort coke. Erin was in the in-crowd of the Orange County legal scene. There were so few of us then that we were tightly knit. Everyone knew everyone. That was the vibe in the late 1980s and early 1990s. That's how it worked.

Add to that mix, that the judge was inattentive. A perfect storm brewed on Magnolia Avenue.

The judge's order, typed by my friend the clerk, read, "It is hereby ordered and adjudged that Mr. Jared Jones sentence of one year in the Orange County jail is suspended, and it is ordered that he spend one day in jail followed by one year of probation." The words "is suspended" meant everything because my client had no jail time to do at all. The power of the two handwritten words kept my guy with his family and working. There was a monumental difference in telling my guy he could go home versus that he would be locked up for a year. You could do this with a vanilla marijuana case like this one but not with rape or child porn or another case where the judge might be more likely to scrutinize the order he signed.

This was the era before gestapo-like courtroom security, cameras, and microphone bugging. Everyone is so nosey now. It wouldn't happen like that today.

Back then, the clerks typed up the court's business in open court memorializing events of the court in court minutes that were mostly drafted by hand. Once the clerk typed orders on paper, she presented it to the judge, and he signed it without reading it. Justice was not always done. It was dicey because what she was doing was illegal but we went with it. We didn't talk about it. It was all communicated nonverbally. Just like with cops creating false evidence in the field, the people inside the courthouse were prone to skirting the rules as well. Once cameras documented every move inside the new Orlando courthouse, this era vanished into Orlando history along with the old building.

I prefer the old human to human method than technology. Nowadays attorneys can hide behind computer keyboards and layers of other barriers to avoid doing real face to face business in practicing law. I'm old-school and prefer a more conventional approach to law where I interact with people. I hate computers and cell phones. When I want a document and paperwork about my cases, I want papers in my hands, not a suggestion to look at a flipping computer screen. I don't like text and e-mails. I want to see and talk to human beings such as the prosecutors, judges, witnesses and, most importantly, my clients the defendants.

This is how we did business in the old courthouse in Orlando, the county seat of Orange County, which was operational until 1997. It was a stark concrete structure on Magnolia Avenue that used to be buzzing with activity and yet it was easy to access. You didn't have to go through airport-style security measures like you do now. In Orlando in the 1980s and early 1990s the population of attorneys seemed small and only a handful of good criminal lawyers were available for hire. Business was done mostly backroom style. Defense lawyers and prosecutors and judges would have vast and substantive discussions about pending cases with an eye on getting them resolved. Judges would take time with each case and talk about the human beings and the impact of their decisions on real individuals.

During those times, the secretaries to the judges, now called judicial assistants, the clerks, and the frontline prosecutors dictated the flow of cases. In contrast, today the flow of cases is dictated by various software programs attorneys plug in to get time in front of judges and get cases moving along the system. The modern-day criminal docket concerns itself with getting cases done without examination of the humans involved. Judges want low caseloads so they try to push the hand of The State and defense to settle quickly without really educating themselves about each situation. The process is reduced to numbers, numbers, numbers! They have no time because of the sheer number of cases today. Also, now those frontline prosecutors can't seem to do much without the say-so of their supervisors. So, now you have a judge that wants you to make a quick decision and a prosecutor who wants to consult his supervisor rather than strike a deal. The system now is bundled with red tape.

So, in earlier decades, when the judicial assistants and the clerks held the cards, smart lawyers did everything to stay in their good graces. With aforementioned Erin, and others of her type, that would mean plying them with food and booze and other party favors around town after hours. We partied at places like Rosie O'Grady's at Church Street Station, Valentine's Jazz Club or Tanqueray's on Orange Avenue, or Wally's on Mills Avenue. There weren't as many choices of bars as there are now around downtown Orlando, but the atmosphere was intense and fun at all of them. Because there were fewer venues, you were sure to see people you knew.

Erin loved to party off the chain. Amazingly, she showed no signs of it when she would spring into court with only a few hours of sleep and proficiently carry out her duties as clerk. She controlled the order in which cases were called and was in charge of summarizing judges' pronouncements so it would be clear to everyone what went down. It was an art form. She worked in a spotlight with people staring at her while she ran the court. She was running the show. We were all in our early careers and out and about. She was attractive and a Good Time Charlie. If she took a liking to you and you became friends it was helpful to get a guy out of jail quicker or get court time. If I could get word to her that I was running late, which meant hungover, she would call my cases last so I would have time to get to court. It was a secret society. She loved to do favors for the drinker-drugger lawyers as we rolled through the court. We all worked hard and played hard.

Eventually she fell off the planet. I wondered whatever happened to Erin. I heard she became a biker chick and started using heavier drugs. I heard a few years later Erin died after succumbing to a pill addiction. A lot of people I knew from that era died. The accounts of family members and obituaries were kindlier and gentler to people who died of drug addiction in describing the cause of death. Oddly enough obituaries would report that people died of natural causes in their sleep. Those of us in the inner circle knew the truth. It was a hard lifestyle to have any hope for longevity.

I feel fortunate that I'm still around given my history with both using and peddling drugs. For too many years I was saturated with drugs and alcohol. It was no way to live. My animalistic party skills created many issues in my life. It became like a job to drink and do drugs and yet somehow function in society. It was a dark chess match daily cycle from the morning terror, through the daytime recovery, to the happy hour joy-joy, to the late night completely toxic alcohol rage. For me, the late 1980s to 1990s were busy and yet blurry.

Being a functioning alcoholic-druggie was a curse. During my younger years, I could stay out until the bars closed, show up to the courtroom for a proceeding half-drunk and half-high, and somehow walk away with incredible results in case after case. My success rate was partly because I felt I was born to be a litigator and partly because I had liquid muscle running through my body which would make me be aggressive in such a way that I would get favorable results.

I was not alone in practicing law by this ill-advised method. A now deceased lawyer was famous in the Orlando courts for showing up in court after consuming several drinks. This brilliant legal mind worked from a house he converted into an office in downtown Orlando. When he prevailed at a trial or got a not guilty verdict, he raised a pirate flag well above his building. That legal pirate character was known to be a more superior litigator drunk than most other lawyers were stone cold sober. He had consistent undeniable successes for his clients. He also had a long rap sheet with dozens of arrests. Back in the day we had badass barristers who spent a little time on both sides of the jailhouse bars.

CHAPTER 7, ST. THOMAS TO STUDY AND SURF

Practicing law between weekend surfing sessions, all the while boozing and drugging, had to start with passing The Florida Bar exam. Getting into the legal field wasn't easy, and later I would find keeping my law license was a bitch at times, too. In the mid-1980s, I failed the Florida Bar Exam twice due to partying, a la JFK Junior, who failed his three times. It turns out The Bar Exam is not an aptitude test. Unless you're a genius you must study and focus to pass. I was not a genius. The fact that I'm certainly not a genius was further evidenced by the fact that days leading up to the Bar Exam in Tampa, I was alternatively going to the Mons Venus strip club at night and the beach during the day rather than attend the Bar Review classes. The Gulf of Mexico on the west side of the peninsula of Florida usually has flat surf. It didn't help that a freak swell brewed in The Gulf in late July, which meant I engaged in surf sessions, not study sessions.

I was not backing off the cocaine and booze and my heart wasn't into studying. I had plenty of money so finances were not a motivator to get my legal career going. My local cocaine dealing was going gangbusters, and at the same time, I was working for law firms as a clerk.

I needed to dry out. I decided it was time for a geographical change so I could clean myself up and pass the exam. Since I was single and nothing was holding me in Florida, I moved root and branch to the U.S. Virgin Islands to get away from the grip of substance abuse. I left my Florida party lifestyle and headed to the Caribbean to a secluded island to study without distractions. It turns out this was a bad, bad move. United States Virgin Islands, or U.S.V.I., was a decadent place. What I was running from on the mainland was waiting on the islands where I was moving. Temptation was hovering and packing power like a hurricane.

I flew into the airport in St. Thomas in a tiny rickety plane where the pilot had to hit the squealing brakes really hard and really fast. That was a foreshadow of Caribbean island life where everything almost works.

I lived with two University of Florida grads. My roommate Sam was a tennis pro and played competitive tennis. His girlfriend's dad was a heart surgeon in Jacksonville. Sandy was a hardcore alcoholic. Sandy being laid-back Sandy, compounded with island time, picked me up from the airport two hours late. As we made our way in her Jeep to the north side of the island to my new residence over Hull Bay, I soaked in the lush tropical landscape. Florida is tropical but the foliage on the islands are more intense in color and size.

My attention was divided between the gorgeous vistas and Sandy driving half-buzzed chattering away on the notoriously poor condition pot-holed island roads. She edged uncomfortably close to the steep cliffs and I was riddled with anxiety because of her inattention to the inherent danger of the steep drop-offs. I was not well traveled, and it was the first time I was in a country where they drove on the left side of the road, too. Upon arrival, I looked out of the back of our rented home overlooking the bay with 1,000 yards of tide pools full of fish and lobster living between sharp coral. There were four-foot perfect right-handed waves shooting across the bay. As a surfer in view of perfect sets of waves, I became completely consumed with the compulsion to paddle out in the bay.

I unpacked into a small closet and I had a mattress on the floor to use. Unpacking didn't take long. My suitcases were broken into in the Puerto Rico airport layover from Orlando and the airport workers stole all of my cool clothes. I had what I needed. I had several shorts and five t-shirts. I had baggies for surfing. I had a few pairs of khakis to wear to the law firm where I would later get a job.

Shortly after arrival, Sandy drove me to the beach. It was 500 yards as the crow flies. In the Jeep, it was a half mile of winding, steep, dangerous roads. Most of the property was private so there was only one way in and one way out of the bay. I stood at sea level, almost a half mile away from the waves, and contemplated how to paddle out through the moored boats anchored in the waters without bothering the boat owners. Also, I needed to figure out any dangers beneath the water such as any sharks, coral, sea urchins or other potential perils. I pushed off the sandy beach after a five-minute assessment and made the long paddle out to the bay where the waves were breaking. Steep sets started to roll in and I was stoked on the surf. I was high as a kite with a natural high.

I met a friendly married couple from San Diego who were happy to share their surf spot. They told me about other breaks down island that I would later get to know very well, Caret Bay and Botany Bay.

We developed a simple yet awesome and fulfilling island life. We speared fresh lobster and grouper and fried it for meals. Life was simple, yet decadent and delicious. We had everything we needed at the time. I drank rum, snorted coke, surfed, and had the time of my life.

The weekend ritual was to visit the beach bars in Tortola in the British Virgin Islands, or B.V.I., which you can see from U.S.V.I. Despite the relatively close proximity, the logistics to get to Tortola were a bit cumbersome but we had it down to a science. We parked the Jeep in Charlotte Amalie around the ferry boats at a jewelry store. We paid the clerk $10 to leave our car overnight in her parking lot. From there, it was a short walk to the ferry where we would grab our ticket for the 45-minute crossing to the stunning B.V.I. in a vessel named the Bomba Charger. It was a two-decker large vessel that transported people and cargo around the little islands comprising the B.V.I. There was a make-shift bar on board for us to occupy our time until we cleared customs at Road Town. The customs process could be swift or painfully slow depending on the mood of the immigration officials. Then we would hire a taxi, which could be almost any make or model vehicle, generally with a little rust, for a 12-minute ride to our first destination, Apple Bay. We paddled out in lukewarm bubble bath water to surf consistent three-foot perfect waves. Apple Bay was home to frisky waves and full moon mushroom parties. Bomba, the proprietor of Bomba Shack next to our surf spot at Apple Bay, had a lazy eye where you never knew where he was looking or to whom he was directing his conversation. After a buzz kicked in, his lazy eye weird-ed me out at times. Like most of the Caribbean bars, Bomba Shack was a ramshackle hut constructed of driftwood and slapped together debris like broken surfboards and pieces of wood with a sand floor. We drank rum concoctions in plastic cups all day on an open tab and when it was time to settle up, Bomba would conjure up a figure out of thin air for us to pay with American dollars. Bomba always discounted my final bill because I gave him little hits of blow during the day. This imbibing took place overlooking breathtaking smooth ridable surf and surrounded by tan beauties in slinky bikinis. The views of water and women created a surfer's Nirvana.

Some people would go to Tortola by private boat but we didn't really need a boat. The ferries got us easily to the other islands. On our island, it would take an hour to get to Charlotte Amalie by boat from our house. It was easier to just drive the Jeep.

By sheer fortuitous luck, on my inaugural plane ride to St. Thomas to make the move, I met a guy who became known to me as Captain Mark.

He and a handful of rich Winter Park, Florida guys were moving to St. Thomas at the exact time as I was. Luckily for me, they had an arsenal of ski boats, jet skis, and other water toys being shipped to the islands. The group had thinly disguised business plans to open a water ski school of sorts. The ski school never really took off but it was a great way to meet whatever single available girls were around, and a good way to make friends. These guys let us borrow their boats to go to remote surf spots, or anytime we wanted or needed a boat. They ended up being a very cool connection.

My University of Florida friends and the Winter Park guys were only the beginning of a big group of us who would share an experience of a lifetime. I was not the only ex-patriot or lost soul who had ventured to this American territory to find something or escape from something. This was more evident as the search for employment commenced. I met people from all over the world who came for adventure, a new start, or just to get away from the mainland.

My roommate Sam was the tennis pro at Bolongo Bay Resort seven days a week. Sandy lined me up a gig as a beach attendant there. I was charged with arranging beach chairs just-so. It was important to thoughtfully place the chairs around the palm trees because nature designed the eight-pound cocoanuts to use gravity to crash hard and plant themselves into the soft sugar sand to grow new trees. I tried to keep the randomly falling tropical spheres from hitting the tourists. I picked up the fallen cocoanuts each morning. There were a lot of palms, a lot of chairs, and a whole lot of fun. Bolongo Bay was as resort-y as resorts get. Everything was available on the property from restaurants, bars, tennis, a marina with boating, and a beach with snorkeling and sailing.

I was also tasked with helping guests onto The Tiki Torch catamaran for sunset cruises. The booze cruise was a drunk-fest where the tourists would come back smashed from drinking rum runners and planter's punch cocktails, with shots of Cruzan rum. The local rum was just a thing. It was sold from every store and restaurant to every roadside vegetable stand. I found it convenient to have rum served everywhere I went.

I also had to take tourists on sailing adventures. I had to learn to sail first. I took naturally to it since I already surfed. The previous two beach attendants taught me how to sail on a little Sailfish. I sailed it out from the resort a few hundred yards and somehow would bring it back safely.

This all was condition dependent. You needed wind. It was easy to get it out but then you had to tack to get it back to the resort. It was fucking insane looking back. I was hired. I was given no formal training and had zero regulations. I was responsible for teaching people to sail in 60-foot-deep water when I did not know myself how to sail. I hoped the tourists could swim. I felt badly that someone knocked their $300 sunglasses in the water. I wished the one guest had not reached her hand out to pet the eel. The crazy resort threw me into the lion's den and didn't give a shit if I knew how to sail or not. They wanted me to just go do it. So, I did learn to sail, and then I did teach tourists what little I knew about sailing. It was island life and I was part of the island culture. The whole adventure was a little amiss, but indeed pure bliss.

Being a beach attendant was without a doubt the best job on the island. Once I got to know the restaurant employees they would deliver free food to me during my shifts. The single girls vacationing on the island of all ages, shapes and nationalities kept the job interesting. The general manager who was an ex-pat from Wisconsin loved to snort coke and tilt his Jack Daniels in the afternoons. He was happy I could be a source of coke and he was fascinated that I was a law school graduate spending my time as a beach attendant. I was fascinated that a man from Wisconsin could speak perfect fluent Patsuay, a Haitian-French-Creole language. Some of the staff spoke this language.

One scene that I will undeniably see when the scenes of this life click before my mind in my last minutes on Earth, was the end of a Saturday afternoon shift. I had been both served and serving rum drinks all day. One might observe I was overserved. I was drunk. The steel band was thumping in the background. I could see tan girls dancing seductively by the pool. I was taking an outdoor shower to rinse off the sand before I got in the pool. The sun-warmed water trickled down with this sensation of peace rinsing my whole body. I was surrounded by stunning girls, surfing, spearfishing and playing tennis. It doesn't sound prestigious to be a beach attendant but it was a pinnacle moment. All I could think was, "I want life to always be like this."

Alas, my beach attendant days ended when I was drunk and high one day and I answered the phone, "Grrrr. Captain Jack here." The voice on the other end answered a bit puzzled, "I'm calling for Jack Wander about a resume he sent to clerk with the Law Office of Trent Taylor." I straightened up, shook off the Captain Morgan rum persona, took the call, aced the interview and was hired on the spot.

Trent was a gay guy out of Philly who was interested in my legal experience. I would figure out that he was much more interested in a sexual relationship with yours truly. I was one in a long line of paralegals working under Trent. I would hear the office manager giggle and snicker when I asked for a coffee mug and a dictation cassette recorder and they were delivered immediately. I assumed those would be normal requests to set up shop in a law office. I would learn that Trent took care of several young gay men around the island. I was not destined to be one of them with my preference for female company. Trent agreeably settled into a professional mentoring role with me. We worked well together and I learned a lot from him about the law. He gave me knowledge and I gave him clients. I brought him a lot of clients by virtue of my ties to the illicit drug community.

The office was near Market Square where back in history slaves were bought and sold. It was situated in a violent place in St. Thomas, and quite dangerous in the night hours. About that time, the crime rate on St. Thomas was among the highest in any U.S. city or territory. Crime was rampant on the south side of the island where the office was, and the whities lived on the north side. The south-island inhabitants were mostly on the government dole, with little resources, and not much opportunity but tourism. It was a rough island, but you would never know it on your two-hour visit walking 500 yards off a cruise ship to buy souvenirs. The reality was that you had to watch where you were and who was around you. My idyllic paradise and illegal peril lived side by side.

CHAPTER 8, MID-1980s AND 8 BALLS IN U.S. VIRGIN ISLANDS

During the idyllic era studying for The Bar Exam, one of the downsides in the Virgin Islands was that local single girlfriend-type ladies were in short supply, other than the tourists rolling through. I had my eye on a local girl but she had a boyfriend named Luke and he was a badass so that option was nil.

In a new surf spot, surfers have to pay their dues before they get any respect whatsoever in the lineup. The lineup is the positioning of surfers in the water just beyond the break vying for the best position to take off for the best waves. After six months getting some traction and some waves, the long-standing locals were ever so slowly warming up to my presence, along with my roommates, who were also surfers from Florida.

Luke was what would be considered the enforcer at Caret Bay. He was clearly the pack leader of the locals and as cold as ice by way of personality. He had a typical surfer look with a tan and a well-built physique, both qualities from hours spent in the water. At the time, we all wore our hair long to our shoulders but not messy like hippies. He had a kaleidoscope head of light brown hair with blonde shiny streaks from the sun and sea. He was tough and aloof and somehow was a chick-magnet after surf sessions.

Luke and his pack practiced strict tribalism around their surf spots. They got in violent fights in the water if someone didn't learn their rules in the lineup or follow their rules. Then the rule offenders might get out of the water to find their car with slashed tires or a cracked windshield. These guys operated like a gang.

As is a theme in my life, I had a fortuitous stroke of luck by being in the legal field as a part-time paralegal at the Law Firm of Trent Taylor in Charlotte Amalie. Surfers in the lineup knew that I worked at the firm. A second stroke of luck came in the form of Luke the enforcer having a small legal problem. It is funny how people don't like lawyers until they need one. The enforcer needed one. As a result, I was spared some of the harsh localism and territorialism.

As a favor of sorts from my boss, we resolved Luke's legal issue within a month. This did not result in the enforcer becoming buddies with me but at least we could converse in the water and surf the same waves. He was a stuck-up asshole. He wasn't pleasant at all but talked to me while I helped him resolve his legal issue. Then, he reverted to ignoring me and not talking at all once he didn't need me anymore. We were vying for the same girl. He was in construction as a painter and I worked for a law firm. St. Thomas was a small island community and those were known facts in our small orbit in the Universe. I didn't know much else about this mysterious character. We would later connect on business ventures, risky business opportunities.

When I wasn't surfing with locals or my roommates, I was looking at surf and longing to surf. I had a picturesque postcard-perfect view with tropical nature as living art with a mix of sun, clouds, birds and ocean tides each day. Sam and Sandy had taken great pains to research and find the most striking vista on the north side of the island. The next bay to the east of Hull Bay, Magens Bay, was a perennial top ten most beautiful beach in the world as reported by National Geographic magazine and travel publications. This view was more mystical to me because I was acutely aware of the cornucopia of waterborne activities both on the water and submerged under the waterline among the coral. I could watch other watermen surfing, fishing, spearfishing, crabbing, lobstering, boating, scuba diving, snorkeling and just chilling on the beach. Hull Bay was a water lover's ultimate playground. Heaven was turquoise. From my vantage point of my balcony in Estate Hull, I could see Inner Brass a small island off St. Thomas on Hull Bay that had consistent perfect right waves that was rarely surfed. Inner Brass surf break was a longer paddle out of about a mile, and more dangerous than the Hull Bay break which was closer to the shore. I would admire the beauty of nature and the perfect swell of both breaks within sight of my dwelling place.

I noticed at the Inner Brass surf spot that two boats would meet and greet regularly. They were not fishing. I could see a small wooden boat that I knew belonged to Luke moor up about twice a month on the eastern tip of Outer Brass Island. I would see Luke's boat and two other boats tied up to one another and at least one would be a go-fast boat. I had a suspicion about drug running.

In the mid-1980s there was a great little drinking joint in the exotic location overlooking the harbor and Charlotte Amalie. Sibs was a hard-drinking spot frequented by locals and occasional brave adventurous tourists. Drinking on the island was ridiculous because the rum Cruzon is manufactured in St. Thomas and was a little over a dollar per bottle. The pineapple juice to mix with the rum cost more than the booze.

On one evening liquid courage set in when I was sufficiently inebriated and convivial. Luke and I had a real conversation. It turned out he was from Melbourne, Florida. He loved surfing at New Smyrna Beach just two hours north of his hometown, and he started to like me a little by virtue that New Smyrna was my home beach. For reasons unknown, I looked up to this guy and wanted him to like me. It was the surf culture and he was the enforcer. I wanted more surf turf and cred in the surf spots.

I had some snort with me and the more drunk I got, I wanted to do a bump or two. I let my guard down and asked if he wanted to partake. His stoic cool-guy guard dropped and he practically leapt off the bar stool so we could ease out to the parking lot and snort some fat lines off the back of his beat-up rusty Datsun pickup. It was on from there. There was a bond if you snorted coke together. It was like a secret society. I became a St. Thomas inner-surfer-circle member at that very moment.

When I travelled to St. Thomas from Florida, I'd bring an eight-ball, which is an eighth of an ounce or three-point-five grams of coke, and split it up with friends and make easy cash profits. People visiting us would also bring an ounce or two and make a few bucks. It's counter intuitive dealing in the small amounts of drugs. The people smuggling coke didn't dip into their stash, so people in the islands were clamoring for party materials to use. The Virgin Islands have a reputation for drug smuggling, so you wouldn't think it would be so hard to get a few lines.

After a few more party sessions at Sibs and a bar called For the Birds, Luke slowly started to let me know he was moving some weight of coke through St. Thomas coming from all over South America, and all over the Caribbean like Cuba and Jamaica. Under the auspices that he hired my law firm, and attorney client privilege, everything he told me was confidential. This cat was moving a decent amount of blow but in the big scheme of things, his operation was small time. There were dealers moving serious weight. Luke was semi-serious. He already had drop offs in Ft. Pierce and Port Canaveral. Over time as I gained his trust, I convinced him to try Ponce Inlet.

He arranged for boats to bring sealed kilos from St. Thomas to the Florida coast. A designated Boston Whaler would motor from St. Thomas to a mile outside of Ponce Inlet between New Smyrna Beach and Daytona Beach where the boat would idle. The boats could conceivably just go into the inlet, but there's a paranoia with smuggling. The theory was that Fish and Wildlife Commission or the Coast Guard were less likely to stop and board a vessel in open water. A boat was much more likely to be stopped and boarded in the calm waters of the Halifax River in the inlet, than in the open ocean where it would be logistically much more of a hassle for authorities. Smugglers do things to avoid detection and also because of superstitions and myths.

After months of discussions and planning with Luke about money matters, a time and date was set for my lifelong friend Bonsai and I to participate in a first exchange. I flew to Florida where at an appointed time Bonsai and I would get on Yamaha jet skis to do the deal.

Before easy to ride wave runners, which were designed and manufactured later, you rode on jet skis. We practiced in all kinds of weather and water conditions. The jet skis were tippy as hell and you couldn't sit until you got some speed. Even at low speeds the jet skis were hard to maintain balance. Wave runners by contrast are like little boats and they don't require athleticism; you just jump on and go. As tippy as the jet skis were, it wasn't advisable to fall with drugs in your backpack. We were extremely nervous about getting the drugs wet and also about the jet skis running properly. The small watercrafts were not new and none of us were mechanical.

For drug exchanges, we got on the jet skis in broad daylight to blend in with the other personal watercraft users and recreational boaters. We took the cash in our backpacks and blew from the dock on the mainland out of the inlet to meet the idling boat a mile offshore. We were becoming drug runners. We were also longtime surfers. We'd lament that we were on jet skis instead of surfing if the waves were favorable in the inlet. We would lust after the waves on both the New Smyrna and Daytona Beach sides as we exited Ponce inlet, committing a major felony.

The scene was helter-skelter like in an action flick. We hoped the guys on the boat weren't cops. We operated on this weird double-blind trust. We would jet ski out with cash, a lot of cash, and throw it on a boat. A guy we didn't like on the boat hands us the kilos. The guys on the boat didn't count the money. We didn't weigh the kilos. It was a quick tense exchange filled with testosterone and adrenaline. The exchange was arranged by Luke. Ignorance is bliss. We didn't ask who the boaters were and they didn't know who we were.

Each time we blew back through Ponce Inlet with the drugs. We then took a hard left into the channel towards New Smyrna Beach, slowed to an idle to not bring attention to ourselves, and pulled up undetected to the small nondescript dock behind an old-Florida 1950s ranch style house. We tied up the jet skis on the dock and came back to get them later after we dumped the blow at our houses or to pre-arranged buyers. A surf rat rented the house and he was happy to accommodate our jet ski antics for a line or two and to be part of the action for the cool factor. The small house on the intercoastal is close to where the popular Outrigger's is now. The vacant land is now a seafaring lovers' multi-purpose venue with a marina, bait and tackle shop, condos, restaurants and a giant inside and outside it-place bar. The whole area surrounding the intracoastal waterway that used to be mangroves and lonely sparse houses is now developed and bustling with maritime activity. There would be too many people today to make that a safe spot for illegal activities.

The first drug exchange was exhilarating, fun and profitable. After that, flying back and forth from Florida to the islands to map out the boat deliveries to Florida became routine. I had a life in both places, and that life included coke.

We mastered the jet skis, but another part of our anxiety was dealing with nature.

One time we had to leave the Boston Whaler with the product on it twisting in the breeze. The waves were too big so we had no way to navigate ourselves out of the inlet. The delivery boaters were surprised that they waited a few hours scanning the horizon for our jet skis that never arrived to grab the product. We pissed off the delivering boat guys because they didn't understand. Before cell phones, we had no way to contact the idling boat a mile offshore. A gruff captain of a small aging vessel who I didn't know and didn't want to know went back to Ft. Lauderdale and unloaded more product on those people than they had the cash to pay. The cranky captain gave the enforcer an earful about me. The dust-up eventually blew over. The captain was not my kind of person. There were many of those characters and I learned to avoid them.

After getting the coke from the boats, we drove from New Smyrna to Orlando to divi-it-up. Once back in Orlando, extreme paranoia set in until all the blow was off our respective premises. The neatly squared keys which we were so hot after, suddenly became hot potatoes. We would frequently get in skirmishes as to who would take extra dope and hold on to it until it was sold. We'd play rock-paper-scissors. Nobody wanted it in their house.

Each of us had calibrated clean triple beam scales that had to be accurate and used with meticulous precision. We were selling tiny particles that were producing extraordinary profits. Every few months, we were getting a few kilos from Luke. The numbers varied but on average we would make around a 30% profit for wholesale. We'd dice and slice some for ourselves. We'd cut a pure coke kilo first into 35 ounces, then some half ounces and quarter ounces mostly designated for lifelong trusted friends. We'd make exponentially the profits if we sold it piecemeal because the smaller the amount, the higher the markup.

In the 1980s people were frenzied to get high quality coke like ours. The folks who bought the dope from our crew would dilute and step on the product so by the time it got to the consumer snorter, it was not nearly as pure as the 98% flake we brought in through the inlet. Typically, the lower level dealers added N-Acetyl that they could get at GNC Stores which had a similar look and texture to coke. So, with a seven-dollar bottle of powder they would add to make one ounce into two ounces and increase their profit by several thousand bucks real-quick-like. The ultimate consumer would get pissed off when they realize how much their coke was being cut. So, low level dopers got more sophisticated. They would mish-mash N-Acetyl with coke and then dampen with acetone which is a colorless flammable liquid, and nuke it in the microwave for a minute. This produced an authentic-looking end product in the bag with consistency of the coveted rock form of coke.

There was a science to it. We had to figure out who you could call and how you would circulate the product discreetly and still market it. We had to figure out logistics before cell phones. It was complicated. You'd start using it. Your friends would start using it. People would knock on your door in the middle of the night. Coke is addictive and people get frantic. It's like you're starving and you have to eat. You want more and more and more. It was all bound to unravel eventually. There were close calls all along the way.

For people in my circle and sphere of influence, this seemed routine and normal. I don't believe it was a secret to anybody what we were up to with our dealing. People talk. People gossip. Interesting information flies quickly. I was mortified one day when my mom came to me in tears. She wanted to talk to me about a rumor. My niece had come home for spring break at Florida State University and went to some local popular nightclubs that I frequented, such as Crocodile Club, JJ Whispers and Spit. I ran into her and we had a few drinks. Apparently after my niece and I parted company, a couple of her girlfriends, who I didn't know, told her I was a coke dealer. She defended me to her friends but being a good kid, she told my mom the word on the street about me. I knew people knew about my dealing but perception and denial are powerful forces. My mom had to know in her heart of hearts the truth. She had been to my apartment and saw the triple beam but chose not to discuss it. Moms know their sons. She knew that I was immersed in coke, both using it and profiting from it. So, I lied. What else would I do? I retorted, "Those girls are full of shit. Yes, I've used it once in a while but a dealer or a dope smuggler, please! I'm working three jobs. What are you talking about?" I was getting ready for my night job at a popular restaurant and bar Raffles in the Altamonte Mall, and I brushed it off as gossip to my mom as I quickly left for work.

Again, our sales were small potatoes compared to what was going on in the cocaine industry. Anyone who sold dope on any level, from kids who sold nickel bags in high school to Pablo Escobar, were lying if they said they did it just for the money. The dope dealer culture in the 1970s and 1980s was the excitement and romanticism of the actual drug running. A good deal of motivation for being in the trade was the adrenaline, machismo and getting away with something. You felt like a character in a James Bond movie. You would have to have a screw loose and be an adrenaline junkie to be in the trade. It was adventurous. Somehow it was more acceptable then, too. I hesitate to claim it was considered cool, but it was.

Glenn Frey of The Eagles captured the vibe in the song "Smuggler's Blues." There are smugglers, sailors, shady characters and dirty deals. The enticement and lure of easy money dealing contraband was hard to turn down for us. Imagine falling into money and making so much so quickly that you have a problem with what to do with the cash. How do you legally have it accounted for in your finances? With the extravagant markups, we had stacks and stacks of cash. My cash box got full constantly at Banco Popular. Then I would convert the cash to checks, then into girthy bank accounts, then convert to purchases of pieces of land on an enchanted island. Each land purchase overlooked a surf break or boat mooring. I was not only living in paradise but buying it, too.

Thankfully everyone used cash then, and less often credit cards. Now some people around that time would bury cash in their yards. That's a foolish idea. The paper currency would rot or inquisitive busy bodies would dig up your bounty. The guy who had the concessions at the Orlando airport around this time tried this tactic and got caught. So, you try to spend your cash. You can only buy so many clothes and dine out and entertain so much. At restaurants and bars, I would tip like nobody's business and leave 100% tip. I'd pay $200 for a round of drinks and wouldn't care. For any situation with any eventual outcome while I was out and about I was loaded for bear. I would pay cash for any type of service. Shit, I paid cash for just about everything including cars. I didn't yet have a professional well-paying job so it wouldn't be hard in those days to figure out what I was up to with my piles of cash. I assumed everyone knew. I wasn't self-conscious about it at all.

In little Central Florida, dope dealers vaguely knew each other, so whether or not we were friendly, we would give a knowing glance when we ran into other dealers. It's hard to explain. There were conflicts but not like mafia type shit. For instance, on one occasion, a kilo was earmarked for an individual who lived in Altamonte Springs. After we went through the gymnastics of getting the blow, we went to his house and he declined to purchase what he had ordered. He already spent his money on a kilo from another dealer. Without even trying, Bonzai and I figured out who the other dealer was and filed it away in our memory banks, nothing more.

I remember one time in New Smyrna Beach at JB's in the 1980s, one guy Nick came up and said hello and laughed that, "The D.E.A. would have a field day in here today." It was funny as shit. I looked around and in every corner of the restaurant was a dealer. We didn't talk about being dealers, but we all knew each other, and were cordial. Every neighborhood has stories of their dope dealers from the 1980s. It was a different time in our culture where drug dealing wasn't as taboo as it became in later decades. As more big international organized crime groups joined in on the drug running to partake in some of the giant profits, our group of surfers and casual dealers got squeezed out. They toted machine guns and attitudes. We had backpacks, fiberglass surfboards, and an insatiable addiction for adventure.

CHAPTER 9, SALES JOB NOT ON THE RESUME

I peddled dope in high school through law school. Ironically, because I was trying to get away from the dope business before I passed The Bar, I got more into it when I moved to St. Thomas. Once I was back in Florida and sworn into The Bar, I was out of the smuggling business. I was still snorting my brains out, though. My law business was taking off beyond my wildest dreams. Getting out of The Trade isn't like on television shows. They don't chase you down because you want to get out. It's not like that at all. You're just one piece of the puzzle. If you're not calling them for an ounce or a kilo, it's just off. It was easy-peasy to end my dealings with Luke and his people.

My time in The Trade was a good source for clients with Italian last names when I got my law practice rolling. I had provided coke to organized crime types from Columbus, Pittsburg and New Haven. The cats had all sorts of contacts for illicit deeds in Florida from Miami to Pensacola. When one of their people got in trouble, they paid up front and in full and demanded that their people come out of their legal entanglements relatively unscathed. A guy I worked with in my drug running life would call that a guy bringing cocaine into Florida got popped in Fort Lauderdale. I'd take care of him. Another guy got popped near New Smyrna Beach. I'd take care of him, too. Lots of calls about lots of guys helped to build my new business. Somehow and incredibly, my misspent youth was paying off in gigantic dividends in my early career.

Selling dope had come naturally for me since I was young. During the time I was growing up and especially in high school, pot smoking was in full vogue.

I was making a few bucks here and there by cutting lawns and delivering pizzas. I happened to tell my friend Bonzai one day that I had a whopping sum of $375 in my bank account. His eyes lit up with an idea.

Bonzai said, "Dude, with that $375 we can get a half pound of weed, cut it up, sell it, and put a lot more right back into your bank account within about ten days."

So, then it was on. I was 17-years-old. Bonzai and I and others in our group would drive to a guy's house by a lake not far from ours. We would wait for the cat to show up parked with our windows down shaded by giant oaks with Spanish moss blowing in balmy Florida breezes. Before technology, we did just the good old sit and wait method of business transactions. We would sit in our cars in his driveway and listen to Molly Hatchett, 38 Special or Pink Floyd on our cassette tape players. The first time I remember driving there in my mom's station wagon. Sometimes the dealer would show up and sometimes not. When we would hear the tires of his heavy Ford truck grind through the gravel driveway, we be both a little nervous and also ecstatic. We would make entry into his rickety ramshackle home hidden in the orange groves and leave with a half-pound. From there, we would go to whosever home was not occupied by parents to weigh the weed, divide it into quarter and half ounces, and package it in plastic baggies to be sold to loyal friends. The smoke would literally disappear within a few days. We would be left with a tidy profit.

During this period of time, small time weed dealing was commonplace. It was "that guy" or "those guys" who provided smoke for the weekend getaways to the beach. I happened to fall into that crowd. There was a dozen or so of us at Foggy Lake High School. That's where the thrill of getting away with something became the secondary reason for slinging the dope. Really, the first reason was to get free weed for ourselves. Small time teen dealers like ourselves took some of our stash for our personal use. Another reason was to put some cash in our pockets. A real strong reason was the camaraderie and the bonding that took place with the transactions.

For fun, we competed for sales. A lifetime buddy nicknamed Leisureman speaks to this day about breaking the sales record on Senior Skip Day in our last days at Foggy Lake High School. He took advantage of my absence while I was in the water. I paddled out to go surfing and by the time I met by my parked VW on the beach three hours later, he sold four ounces of weed out of my car. We were thrilled and laughed for weeks about his beachside bounty as one of our last high school highlights. Leisureman would later use those honed sales skills in his career as a sales professional.

Teens at that time held keg parties at their homes when their parents were absent. Verbal news of the events was shared at the beach or at school. Of course, my parents would never have approved of parties at our house and they always seemed to find out about them. For example, a burn on the linoleum kitchen floor gave evidence of one kegger. They didn't get too steamed up about it. I guess they likewise found ways to socialize with other teens in their youth.

Weed evolved into coke. Before one particular kegger at my house, I was a beer drinker and pot smoker. I threw a party for myself for my 17th birthday. A friend called me to the dining room table while the party was kicking into high gear. This was going to be the very beginning of a very tumultuous road laid out before me for decades to come. He laid out four small white lines with a razor onto the glass topped table, and said, "Here you go birthday boy." He wrongly assumed that I had snorted coke before. I didn't want to fess up to being a virgin so I watched him as he snorted the first line and took note. I took the straw from him and snorted the next half inch line into each nostril. Uncertainty quickly dissipated into euphoria. I thought, "Wow! I am a born substance abuser! This is awesome!" With the flip of a switch, a shy, mellow kid, lacking in confidence became mega-self-assured and conversant and quite the ladies' man.

I had many omens in my life as it relates to alcohol and substance abuse. One such omen appeared one hour after I snorted that first line. A soccer teammate cornered me later at the party and in the most serious tone confronted me about using those hardcore drugs with the most concerned and incredulous look on his face.

He demanded, "Why would you do drugs with all you have going for you? It's so stupid. It will be your undoing."

This foreshadow would be one of several omens that haunt me to this day. I didn't listen. I would learn the hard way that drugs would damage many aspects of my life.

CHAPTER 10, OMENS OF FUTURE ALCOHOLISM

My name is Jack and I'm an alcoholic. If I had a dollar for every time I uttered that phrase, I could live in a Caribbean plush mansion. In the Alcoholics Anonymous program, or trying to stay in the program, I picked up a white chip every time I had a relapse. I fell off the wagon so many times that I could tile my mansion floor with little white chips. I got it bad. Dancing in the background of all of my ill-advised behavior through the years is alcoholism. At times when I would get to the other side of ravenous addiction through the AA program, life was generally rewarding and joyous.

There were several things in my youth I never dreamed would be part of my adulthood. One was not a dream but rather a nightmare, alcoholism. For those afflicted, each brand of alcoholism is unique. Thoughts and opinions about alcoholism and alcoholics vary greatly from the gentler school of thought that alcoholism is a disease to the harsher theory that alcoholics are weak and morally corrupt. Some middle of the road people may chalk up alcoholic behavior to stress or trauma.

I believe alcoholism is genetic. I see it sprinkled through both sides of my family tree, but more heavily weighted on the maternal side. About 80% of my mother's side of the family is social, functional, successful, and leading normal lives. The afflicted ones are not spoken of much. They don't show up at family gatherings or reunions. Some are as sad as living in their vehicles until they can shoot up more heroin. Others may have housing but little interest in family interactions, partly because they are too drunk or too high. Several are mentally so beat down they merely want to stay home and imbibe, or they are healing from crazy escapades from previous addictive incidents. It's obvious who has the alcoholic gene.

My brand of alcoholism is colorful, obvious and end-stage. I had omens of my oncoming alcoholism from a young age. Burned into my brain is an image of a man driving an antique two-door Ford pickup on a lonely dirt road in Pickett County in Tennessee. I was six-years-old and I still recall every detail. My parents were driving us to a relative's home and we passed this old country man. He was driving much slower than us and veering off of his lane. As my father navigated past a clunker truck, I looked to the right to see a ghost of a man clutching his steering wheel fighting to stay on the road. He had an old farmer's hat tilted back with a tuft of grey hair poking out of the hat like straw. His skin was a grotesque green-grey hue smudged with alcohol induced slimy sweat. In addition to his dusty grime and look of terror, the prominent facial feature was his deep swollen purple bags under his eyes. Something inside of me ached from the sight of this old guy. I learned of the man's state when my mother whispered to my father, "Lord, that looks like he's on a week-long bender."

My mom's father was a bootlegger from the Prohibition Era so she had personal knowledge of alcoholics and their stages. My mom was from a poor family from a small town in Tennessee not too far from where we were driving when I had this epiphany. They were dirt poor and never owned a home. They were always on the run from creditors. My grandfather had no formal education and didn't make it through high school. He would resettle with his family in urban areas of Ohio always with whiskey on his breath. I found him cold yet kind. Men of that era weren't brought up to be soft like they are today. My grandparents lived on a farm by the time I came along. In Cincinnati on the east side were the up-and-comers like my parents. On the west side were Tennessee shit-kickers with no education and no manners. On that west side is where I would visit Grandpaw and Grandmaw on their farm to climb apple trees, ride ponies and hang tobacco. My grandfather had a barn there where he could fix anything. He'd work on his Chevy pickup, tilt back his flask of homemade whiskey, then go about his business. I'm pretty sure that is where I got the alcoholic gene.

My DNA history of my family and my psyche converged. My mom's whispered words and some primitive survival mechanism inside of me was firing off a warning shot into my elementary school age brain in the back of my dad's car. I can't explain my vivid recollection of the memory of this stranger in any other way. The same holds true for another omen, six years later with another alcoholic man.

I went for a weekend with a school friend and his sisters to his lake house on a lake in Michigan. We had a blast on the lake water skiing and swinging from rope swings to plop into the lake. We explored in the creeks and searched for Petosky stones.

Mark's dad by day was sober and pulled us around the lake at the helm of his ski boat, prepared our meals, and played the dad role. When the clock struck 5 o'clock, he started mixing cocktails. Us kids were oblivious until the 7 o'clock hour. His dad's behavior changed radically for the worse in front of wall-to-wall teenagers. He would make lurid comments about his daughter's friends. His vulgar speech slurred. When he tried to get my attention once, he screamed something unintelligible and pinched my leg leaving a bruise. By about 9 o'clock, the adult friends would hand carry the dad to his bedroom for him to pass out. The odd part of this weird weekend is that the other kids acted as if they didn't notice the off-color behavior. The adults acted as though it was routine, because it was. The other kids ignored his offensive comments and avoided going near him. Everyone in attendance at the lakeside weekend just accepted matter-of-factly that the dad was a drunk and that is just how life was with him.

I had never been exposed to anything of this magnitude. The personality light switch phenomenon was both frightening and mesmerizing. Instead of ignoring the dad, I couldn't detach my attention from his behavior. How could a man go from being a normal dad to a monster in a few short hours? The metamorphosis of this fun-loving dad to this incorrigible man through alcohol burned into my brain with the terrifying premonition, "That is you in 20 years."

A third omen etched into my mind would happen later in my teen years when I was a lifeguard with my YMCA lifeguard license at Wekiva Springs State Park in Apopka, Florida. The 72-degree water pumps out of the underwater springs year-round regardless of weather and is a mecca to escape the heat of Central Florida. I was a lifeguard at one of the deep-water places where the water is basically still. Most days I would be sitting under the shade looking at girls.

After one shift, a destitute-looking older man with leathery dried sunburned skin in ragged jean shorts was convulsing on the ground surrounded by empty Bud tallboy cans. He was going through alcohol withdrawal and found himself on an island with no alcohol, balled up in agony. Passersby looked at him with disdain and ignored his plight and said, "He's a drunk. Just leave him there." This man looked like he was dying. Nobody called 911. I didn't either. I just breezed by like the others. At that time, I still looked with disdain upon fellow human beings who could not control drinking enough to maintain themselves and to function. I was appalled, along with the others, that this man was so out of his mind in a public park in the afternoon. I know now he was detoxing badly and in desperate need of alcohol. He was moaning clearly in grave discomfort and shivering on a 100-degree rocky ground with his arms and legs pulled up to his body convulsing and tensing.

This seven-second image was burned into my memory by a higher power just like the first two omens. The detail of this person's pathetic state came with a message from above, "Better watch it. Look for a solution. Don't be judgmental. Those people are really sick ... and so are you."

There is something spiritual in the nature of man that warns us through omens. These three significant omens didn't save me from my alcoholic destiny, neither did the omen from my soccer teammate when I first snorted coke. The mental images did stay with me in my consciousness each and every time I would have an alcoholic episode. There would be many episodes, so very many. I wondered so many times if I could have changed the course of my destiny.

CHAPTER 11, FROM OHIO TO A FLORIDA "HIGH" SCHOOL

Part of my destiny was to bend rules. My mischievous behavior was evident at a young age. My smile, good nature, top grades and sports participation camouflaged many of my youthful misdeeds.

My father likewise was a bit of a renegade. In our basement, he set up lead bullet traps for us to shoot BB guns, pellet guns and 22 caliber rifles. He let us kids shoot with him.

The old man also was a pioneer in the sense that he built a solo cabin on top of a mountain on a lake in northern Tennessee. The land around the cabin would later be developed into a neighborhood. We spent much of our summers and holidays hunting, fishing, camping, riding motorcycles and exploring nature around the expansive acreage. My father was somewhat danger-indifferent. Like many kids my age at that time, by about eight-years-old, I would go boating by myself, or sometimes with friends my age, and explore all day without checking in with my parents. It was a rather carefree upbringing from that vantage point.

Without staunch parental supervision, coupled with my tendency towards trouble, I was frequently being disciplined. Back then, parents disciplined their children unlike today's generation who tries to talk and reason with their kids. I'd often get spanked or get sent to my room as a result of my missteps. My room was my refuge. I had a Panasonic radio, that in secret during my time-out, I'd put on an AM sports station to listen to Cincinnati Reds. If I couldn't get away with playing the radio, I read books of biographies. I especially gravitated to Daniel Boone, Davy Crockett, Chief Tecumseh and other characters from the pioneer days in early America. Reading those books, I am convinced set a foundation for my vocabulary and speech patterns that would help me immensely later in life as a litigator. I spent a lot of time in my own little world because I just couldn't follow the rules. It never struck me that I had to follow all the rules. I wouldn't think twice to break a rule. I followed the ones I felt were important. I hurt only myself by my rule breaking I learned as I matured.

I practiced my rule bending where I grew up, in an idyllic upper-middle-class safe Midwestern neighborhood on the outskirts of Cincinnati, Ohio. My neighbors had 12 children around my age. We had an instant team for sports. We also pulled pranks which were common at that time. We would shoot glass bottles with BB guns to watch them shatter. We would put dog poop in a paper bag, put it on a doorstep of a neighbor's house, light it on fire, ring the doorbell and run. We would hide behind hedges and throw snowballs at oncoming traffic. We would shoot my dad's rifle in the basement into the bullet trap when he wasn't there. We often got caught.

I lived in that home until I was 15-years-old. I was an immature 15. In 1975, my father, who was successful in the insurance business, announced we were moving to Florida. In short order, I was piled in the backseat with my younger sister in my mother's 1970 Chevy station wagon on the two-day drive to Sweetwater Pines in Longwood.

I was mentally and emotionally lost. My dozen dear friends were no longer next door. I did not know a soul and I was not outgoing or gregarious. After kicking around the house a few days, I gravitated to the common denominator ever present in my world which was the lure of sport. I moseyed up to the tennis courts. Pretty quickly to my great surprise and joy, I met new friends. They were new to the area, too, and welcomed new friendships. Some of them would turn out to be lifelong close relationships.

One of the lifelong persistent friends I met at the sports complex in Sweetwater Pines was booze and drugs. When offered my first joint, which was my first interaction with illegal drugs, I put up a pretense that I had gotten high before and started toking. I wanted to fit in with my new friends. I wanted that sense of community and belonging that I had in Ohio. I took my first toke of weed. It was love! I went from shy to conversant and outgoing within minutes. This was the beginning of my coming out of my shell with the aid of chemicals. I would continue my pattern of fitting in with the other teenagers by going deeper into drugs by trying coke and testing dealing dope. Each personal experiment would take off like rockets. Ka-boom! I was hooked.

Within the first week, my other new friend who would later be nicknamed Weasel-D had swiped a six-pack of beer from his pop. He also swiped a bottle containing a mixture of vodka, bourbon and gin. The concoction was the genius result of the plot to steal liquor from the parental units and not be caught. Again, bowing to peer pressure per usual, I turned up the bottle of the wicked, nasty concoction. I only ingested a shot and almost vomited as a result. Somehow, I kept it down and amazingly and remarkably everything, and I mean everything, in the world seemed right. I suddenly had friends who admired my tennis skills, pretty girls who wanted to get to know me, and I suddenly felt on top of the world. The deep and meaningful relationship, trust and unconditional love between booze and I was cemented. In very rapid fashion, I went from reserved with the outward appearance of being arrogant, to a friendly, talkative, social Central Florida teenager.

Where just days before my only thoughts were negative about the move to a new state, I was now ecstatic. From this day of my introduction to mind altering substances, it seemed that I woke up now to a clear purpose – to get out in the world and get high. Partiers beget partiers. News and gossip travel fast in these little communities. So, quickly I fell into the group of kids who liked to use and I collected like-minded friends quicker than you could say Sweetwater.

By the time I was in my first year at Foggy Lake High School just a few months later, I was getting high before, during, and after school. Any other high school student who moved to the Florida school systems during the mid-1970s, will confirm that the academics in Florida schools at that time were somewhat of a joke. Many of us moved from the Midwest and the Northeast where academics were more stringent. A-rated grades were ridiculously easy to come by whether I was higher than downtown Orlando's CNA Tower or not.

CHAPTER 12, TRADED MIDWEST FOR FLORIDA'S WILD WEST

Getting good grades at my new school was a breeze compared to my prior midwestern education. Something also wildly different about Florida was school sports. I made the high school soccer team. That would not have happened in places where soccer had already put down roots as a serious international sport. Competition to get on a school team would have been much fiercer. I had a healthy dose of paranoia and insecurity as a teenager. My soccer team involvement helped boost my self-esteem through participation in high school sports. Not only did I make the team in Florida but I was a starter. We had a high skill level soccer team, all small and very fit. In my senior year, we placed third in the finals in the state championship games held in Miami.

Similar to the rest of the student body, 80% of those boys on the soccer team liked to drink and get high as well. This little move to the peninsula of Florida was not only working out but by this time I figured I'd hit the jackpot. Florida was teen party mecca in paradise.

It was an exciting time. The Sweetwater Pines license plates became a status symbol in Central Florida. Sweetwater was the "it" neighborhood. Families from all over the states were invading big urban sprawling developments in Central Florida. Because of Florida school bussing policies at that time, Florida-based families also flocked to the newly developed upscale suburbs like Longwood, or alternatively sent their kids to private schools.

Central Florida was one big melting pot. Everyone was new at the same time. That had a lot of pluses. The neighborhoods and houses all looked similar and so did the people. Most of the students had a similar socio-economic and ethnic background. I remember that everyone got along pretty well. I don't remember gangs, or mean girls, or the excessive bullying that are in schools today. Graduating classes at Foggy Lake High School at that time approached 1,000 students before another local high school was built in 1981 to absorb the rapid growth of Seminole County. So, there were a lot of kids but it was easy to socialize in the various social groups like the partiers, the athletes, the surfers, the rah-rahs, the nerds, and the smoking area kids. We had a smoking area on campus and it was packed between classes with kids firing up cigarettes and joints. Many of us were in several of the loosely defined social groups. We all melded and flowed easily with each other.

Florida was the Wild West in terms of partying. The newly relocated teenagers were all having tremendous fun. We had massive keg parties on undeveloped properties off of Markham Woods Road which parallels Interstate 4. Those large acre lots now have sprawling homes on them. We also had parties at kids' homes when their parents were out of town. Some of the kids were making pretty good money charging admission to their under-age drinking parties.

We also went to Rosie O'Grady's in downtown Orlando. The door attendants didn't seem to mind the driver's licenses, which were obviously fakes or belonged to an older sibling. The drinking age at that time was 18-years-old so the appearance of a 16-year-old could easily pass as a legal drinker. If kids got pulled over, the cops would usually give a warning and tell drivers to go straight home, as long as they were coherent enough to give the cops the real driver's license and not the fake one.

Central Florida was transitioning from a sleepy agrarian community, which had the last economic and growth surge for engineering in the 1950s, to a large multi-faceted metropolitan. The police hadn't made the transition at that time to handle the larger population. It was still good-old-boys running the area and policing the streets. Mothers Against Drunk Driving hadn't yet started their assault on under-age drinking, that would strike in 2007. As the heat rose from political activist groups on law enforcement and drinking establishments, the drinking age rose to 21. Partying in high school and college would therefore would have to be more strategically planned for future young Floridians.

The community support like policing, education and all the infrastructure got planned after the housing developments were built in the 1970s. Families moved to enormous developments. The urban sprawl and rapid growth of the post-Disney 1970s forever changed the dynamics of the Central Florida community. In Ohio, streets and parking were well organized and planned to get you to places smoothly. By contrast, the Florida Department of Transportation built haphazard reactionary solutions that morphed into the concrete hell-scape we live in now. The Interstate 4 multi-lane construction-ridden, bottlenecked, twisting crash course slicing right through the center of Greater Orlando is the most highly visible result of the lack of planning or disastrous planning at best.

I've wondered what it might have been like if I stayed in the Midwest. I was so insular. I had my friends. I would have gone to Ohio State. I like the idea of Midwest values, with practicality, substance, organization and rules. Instead, as fate would have it, I left the Mayberry of Ohio for the Mayhem of The Sunshine State. In Florida, the infrastructure was weak. The school structure was flimsy. This left a lot of wiggle-room for a teen ready to be a part of the world, particularly the party world. Loose ends equal loopholes. I left perpendicular perfect squares in all aspects of life with pragmatic predictability, and headed straight into short cuts, detours and dead ends. Racing full speed ahead, with the gas pedal pushed firmly down on the pot-holed disorganized asphalt Florida roads, I left the Midwest for The Wild West.

CHAPTER 13, THE SURFING SWITCH TURNED ON

My father moved us to Florida for his career, but also for the sunny weather and the water. So, he was soon fishing at the coast on weekends. I was soon surfing.

The first wave I ever rode till its conclusion was beyond surreal! I rode a stomach-high wave about 60-feet on a small beach break at New Smyrna. This surfer was turned on! I looked around proudly to see who was watching my great feat of athleticism and I had no audience. My dad was looking down rigging his fishing gear and my mother was tending to my younger sister giving her a fresh water shower from a gallon milk jug filled with water brought from home. The other surfers in the water didn't know me nor did they care. Once I caught my breath I didn't care who was watching. With my addictive personality, I was so deeply hooked and firmly focused on one thing only for the next four hours. I rode four more stellar waves that day which is mediocre, but in my mind, I reigned supreme over the liquid playground. I'm quite certain my style was awkward and the speeds I achieved on my surfboard were probably about a fraction of what I had branded into my brain.

The board was a pawn shop purchase for $15. My Pops had purchased it for my 15th birthday. It was a piece of crap, which is probably the best way to learn the sport. Since I didn't have the luxury of a sleek new board that floated well, turned well or caught waves with ease, I had to study the movements of the water more closely. The dinged-up waterlogged cracked fiberglass board made it difficult for me to figure out how to harness the strength of the little Florida waves. I had to really concentrate and study the water to figure out the physics, balance and weight shift to turn the piece-of-crap surfboard. My single fin Freedom board was only a thrifty bargain board but nonetheless my first love, and I was deeply in love.

One of the reasons I had this over a ding-free new twin fin, which was all the rage at the time, was my Pops was cheap. He was never one to buy expensive sports equipment for us kids until he knew we would stick with the sport. I had been begging for the board for a while. Thanks to everything that is Holy, he actually did see me enthusiastically riding some of those first few waves. My parents were attentive parents and they knew their children well. Based on the duration of my stay in the water that day, the bright red sunburn on my back, and the euphoria in my blue eyes, they knew that I'd take up surfing in earnest. In short order I became proficient.

Since that memorable day, the addiction has only grown. There is no off switch for this lifelong recreational sport. Surfing pops up in my current life playing pickleball, I'll hear my surfer friend yelling from the back of the court in a language only us surfers know. Surfing has dictated a good piece of my life such as where I traveled, where I lived, and with whom I chose to spend time.

CHAPTER 14, SURF LESSONS FROM A SURF SNOB

Tourists in Costa Rica, Hawaii, The Virgin Islands, Mexico or California rarely do a paddle out of Nosara, Waikiki, Hull Bay, Cabo or Malibu and gaze back at the land. I find it to be a wildly unique perspective to experience and savor these destinations from a water view on a surfboard. I can't imagine spending the time and funds to plan a trip around a coastal area and not paddle out to see the panoramic view from the water. If I don't surf at a destination where there's an ocean, I feel like I haven't even been there. It would be like traveling to Florida and going to only the themed attractions. You would miss so much of the intrinsic beauty of Florida life.

I like to travel with surfers or I end up surfing by myself. Countless times throughout my life near home or when I travel, people express an interest in learning how to surf. At the Florida beaches you can see people gracefully riding the crests of the waves. Who wouldn't want to try to surf?

I've also encountered countless people who said they had surfed but they quit surfing. Like so many things in life – athletics, jobs, relationships, and other human endeavors can be made to look easy, but they are not. Golf and tennis are great examples. One can watch the PGA tour and see the players with perfect form smack a golf ball 300-yards at their intended targets, and it doesn't look that difficult. They have a smile and no sweat. Take a novice though, and without a lot of instruction, practice and discipline, the balls are going to be sprayed in all directions. Learning to surf is like golf in that it is an individual sport and depends upon the individual to get past the frustrations of the learning curve to the thrills of actually enjoying the sport.

Over the years, a lot of people such as neighbors, fellow lawyers, friends and family have expressed an interest in learning to surf. When I was a younger single guy on the prowl, females often asked flirtatiously or drunkenly, "Can you teach me to surf?" In the early years, I would be agreeable knowing it would never happen. Then my rote answer got a bit complex. I would tell them, "No, I cannot teach you how to surf but I can help you teach yourself how to surf." Like many things in life worth pursuing, one has to learn through direct hands-on experience of trial and error.

Folks don't like that response. People want to think that pursuits like surfing or lawyering or other endeavors of high intrigue have a blueprint or direction manual to follow. There is not. While there are certain basics like picking equipment, where to have the first surf session, how to paddle and how to catch waves, learning to be a proficient surfer is actually complex.

First of all, you have to be super comfortable in the ocean. That usually knocks out 50% of would-be participants. Most normal people, and rightfully so, will preoccupy themselves with the notion of the stingrays, jellyfish, barracuda, crabs and sharks just below the water's surface that are just waiting to rub up against you and take a little nip. In New Smyrna, a surfing capital, of course the critters are swimming around like every ocean. The water tends to often be churned up with sand giving less visibility to sea life and increasing the possibility of an encounter. When the surfing candidate is pushing the board out to the breaking waves with a preoccupation of sea critters, it will often dampen their enthusiasm to become a surfer. Some still paddle out and give a half-hearted effort.

A newbie can look out and see the whitewater after the wave has broken and see it as an aesthetic frothy aftermath of a breaking wave. Another 25% of candidates fairly quickly get dissuaded at the notion of surfing because they get smacked by that salty pretty whitewater. The whitewater has quite a bit of force and will knock you back with vigor if you don't know how to negotiate it. Just getting out past the break so you can catch the waves before they break can be exhausting. On many days, the sport is more paddling than surfing. You don't ride the whitewater. You ride the swell before it breaks.

If not remaining cognizant of the location of the surfboard, it inevitably will smack surf students in the face, head, arms and legs further decreasing the enthusiasm of the would-be wave rider. The fiberglass fins can be sharp and can cut surfers. An experienced surfer knows to point the nose of the board at the oncoming whitewater to give the force of the water less to grab. Once on the board and paddling, especially with a tall wall of whitewater, surfers learn to duck dive by pushing the nose of the board under the whitewater and trying to swim under it. Experienced surfers get knocked around, bruised and cut even with knowing the tricks.

For the last 25% of the would-be surfing population, those that conquer their fears and muster the physical stamina and skills to get to the actual surf break, they then can teach themselves to surf. It's best to get a feel for the board and how it moves through the water by laying on it first in shallow water and paddling back and forth until the surf student learns where on that board is best for their body to achieve the best balance. Then when they get the gumption, they can try to paddle towards the shore and get the sensation of paddling in the motion of the rolling water. Near the shore it might just be the movement of the tide rolling towards shore. Surf students need to use caution falling from boards during the potential wipe outs in the shallow water. Falling on the sand bottom below can cause neck and back injuries in rare cases.

The next step is to get out to the break. It's easy to tell where the break is if you are in a surf spot because that is where the lineup will be. The lineup is where the surfers are sitting or lying on their boards waiting for waves. Lots of sheer experience is the only way to learn how to read oceanic conditions and to anticipate the action of waves. Before one stands up, the wave has to give sufficient momentum to give time to stand up on the board. Surfers grab the side rails of the board and lift their bodies until their feet are on under them on the board. Where do the feet go on a board? The surfer decides ahead of time which foot to put forward. Left foot forward is regular and right foot forward is called goofy foot. Both are acceptable. The leash is attached to the back ankle, and this would have been done on shore. Goofy foot surfers prefer to take off on waves that break from right to left so they can face the wave and regular foot surfers prefers prefer the opposite break. Facing the wave makes riding the wave more productive, easier and enjoyable. The surfer also has to decide in advance whether to ride the wave to the right or to the left. Watching the sets roll in will help the surfer determine whether the waves are breaking to the left or to the right. The surfer will shift the weight of his or her body and push on the board to direct it where to go on the rolling edifice of water.

There are several certainties of a surfer's first attempts at surfing. One of the certainties is that they are going to take off on some waves with their weight too far forward. This will cause the nose of the board to dig straight in the water and the surfer will be launched forward involuntarily with their extremities flying in every direction. This is called "over the falls" or pearling and others will surely laugh at you. The surfer will feel the leash pull on the attached ankle and this will indicate which way is up towards oxygen. If the surfer is lucky, they won't hit their head on the board coming up and if they aren't kicking too hard, the board might not torpedo back towards them.

Another certainty is that the novice surfer will situate their weight too far back on the board. This is common after going over the falls a few times and fear kicks in to the candidate. Paddling into waves too far back on the board will result in catching zero waves because paddling in that fashion makes it impractical for the board to garner the momentum needed to paddle into the wave. Newbies in this predicament get exhausted and upset and out of breath as they watch the experienced surfers catch and ride the waves in a way that is second nature. This is about the time that 20% of future surf aficionados give up, so now we're down to 5%, of not the whole population, but only those that express an interest in surfing.

When a new surfer in the lineup does start paddling to catch a wave, it is very important to be aware of where the other surfers are, if they are paddling for the same wave, and which direction they will surf. Keeping a safe distance is important for the safety of all the surfers especially while a new surfer is learning to control the board. This is where the concept of cred comes into play in the lineup. Typically, locals of that surf break or more experienced surfers get the first pick of each set of waves. It's the unwritten but globally practiced social protocol. New surfers can watch the more experienced surfers for tips on style and form if they get nudged out of wave opportunities. More ideally, new surfers would engage an experienced surfer and practice with them at a less crowded break.

Then there are the naturals. The rare few true believers in the sport and the lifestyle. These are the apprentice surfers that are so determined, so single-minded that they are going to catch a wave. They are going to put all the ingredients together in just the right way, with just the right timing, that they will experience one of the most sought after, unique, spiritual experiences known as riding a wave. Then, once they have that first magical thrill of actually surfing, they do what every surfer does, they paddle back out again ... and again.

CHAPTER 15, THE MINNOW SURFS MAFIA HOUSE

In my early days in the surf culture, I earned an embarrassing moniker. Most surfers and surf spots had a nickname. Surfer slang was the predominant language in the water. We shared a love of surfing and also a communication style. My crew has ridden waves together for decades. We share our collective memories and acutely honed knowledge of our surf spots, the wind, tides, and all the other forces of nature affecting surf sessions. After countless experiences, sometimes with struggles and other times pure fun, we had our surf routines down.

On an exceptionally large swell for Florida in our teen years, my friends and I scouted a beach break in front of a New Smyrna party spot called The Mafia House. South Atlantic Avenue at that time was desolate sea dunes except for one lone abandoned estate. The steel-reinforced blocky multi-story estate was commonly thought to have bullet-proof windows, underground pistol range, rooftop heliport, and rooftop gun mounts, all hidden behind significant fencing. Before the internet, you couldn't look up the history of a property. Rumors sufficed as fact. A moneyed owner purchased over 100-acres in the late 1960s, but the source of the man's wealth was hazy. The real mystique for locals was in his death. His obituary was public. According to newspaper articles, he was found dead at the bottom of a sand dune on his property where his tractor had apparently fallen on him. For circumstances unexplained, a revolver was found close to the body with several spent shell casings. After a thorough 1970s-style investigation, no foul play was unearthed. With scintillating stories swirling, thrill-seeking teens flocked to the public beach in front of what we called Mafia House for fun, surf, beer, drugs, sex, and to catch a glimpse of the proof of the rumors to solve the mystery. Many Floridians knew the Mafia had partnered with local developers and built large estates and golf courses sprinkled all throughout Florida for wealthy disreputable northerners to escape the cold winters. So, The Mafia House was a viable label for the ominous edifice. Driving along the 13-mile beach, it was a landmark spot for teens to gather. We were among them on one memorable day.

Between wave sets, we sat on our boards for long periods of time and had to entertain ourselves, so nicknames emerged then evolved. One poor friend ended up with Weasel-D. He had an indentation in his chest that even though he was muscular and fit, the indentation was obvious. We cruelly referred to it as a tropical depression, which evolved to Tropical-D, and somehow to Weasel-D.

Another surfer who by most accounts was a good-looking kid, had thick curly hair. It would be coveted today, but in the 1970s, it was worn long like all of us with straighter hair, but his was piled up on his head. It gave the impression from some angles of the trusses on top of a poodle. In contrast to his rich brown locks, his teeth were healthy and very white and protruded somewhat resembling the mouth area of a rodent. So, depending upon the day and what angle we looked at him, we referred to him as The Poodle, The Rat or The Mouse-like Creature.

Weasel-D, The Rat and I were surfing for hours one day at this hot spot in front of Mafia House. The waves were breaking just overhead 200-yards from the beach. By Florida standards, the waves were outstanding. Florida waves are more typically just two to three-feet. The sets were coming in with long periods between sets so if you caught a wave and rode it the 200-yards towards shore, you could time the paddle back out with relative ease between sets. A two-wave set came by and The Rat took the first wave and Weasel-D the second. I was left sitting past the surf break waiting patiently for the next set. I was scanning the ocean looking at my friends in the distance paddling back out towards me.

It was summer and we were frolicking in the bathwater temperature Atlantic Ocean. Before sunscreen and rashguard sport shirts were widely used, to cool off a bit from the sun, we submerged ourselves in the water. I grabbed the rails, or sides, of my board and thrust myself several feet into the water, to float and relax. My bright yellow with orange graphics Natural Art pintail shortboard peacefully bobbed beside me while I took a quick dip. When I came up and put my forearm on the board to pull myself back up, I could now see my friends paddling towards me 20-yards away. The second I spotted them, they stopped paddling, sat up on their boards and started yelling, "Jack, watch out!"

Just as their words filled the air, something hit my thigh hard. I never saw it. Whereas in some South Florida surf spots and in the islands off the coast of Florida, the water is clear and you can see to the bottom, at New Smyrna the water often has less clear visibility. I saw nothing. I immediately jumped up on my board and paddled to shore. Actually, I don't remember paddling, but seemed like I was flying as I willed myself to the safety of the beach. I flew by my friends. When I got to the sand, I ripped my leash off of my ankle and threw my board down in the sand. I proclaimed, "That's it! I quit surfing!"

When they paddled up behind me they were visibly shaken. While they were paddling out, they saw not one but two large shark fins headed directly at me. Sharks are all over New Smyrna, swimming below the surface where you don't see the fins. This encounter was unusual because of the size of the pair. We could rationalize that "our" sharks wouldn't hurt us but these were a different sort and we assumed they didn't know our local protocol for shark-no-surfer-eating etiquette.

My right thigh looked like someone had rubbed sandpaper on the skin. I had been hit by the coarse nose of a large shark but not bitten. From that day on, I was dubbed The Minnow. This name does not instill romantic notions with the girls, nor does it demand respect from other surfers. Before that shark encounter some surfers called me The Mini Hoi-Hoi Creature after little dolls around that time that had long white hair attached to their heads. They thought the dolls had a resemblance to me.

As if my new lame label were not embarrassing enough, it seems all of the locals were around to witness my trauma and my swearing off of surfing. Boxer and Bonsai were parked next to us on the sand beach. Surf Puppet, Weird Beard, Surf Cowboy, Zip Brad and The Old Man longboarder all got an earful of my declaration to stop surfing. Even The Poser watched my sad state. The Poser still had dry hair, of course. He didn't surf but was one of those guys who tried to look cool parked on the beach with his board strapped into the surf racks. For a short moment, even this hardcore surf addict thought the non-surfers might be smart for staying out of the damn shark-ridden waters.

I did quit surfing that day. By this era, surfing and my crew were an integral part of my life so my abstinence lasted less than an hour. I paddled back out to the waves. My friends wouldn't let me sit on the beach with epic overhead waves within view. The waves were unusually big and good form for Florida. The sharks were big, but the waves were big, too.

After our surf session, we hopped back in our cars piled high with boards on top for the hour drive back to Longwood, through the two-lane State Road 44, to Interstate 4. We drove after taking Quaaludes and washing them down with keg beer. On the drive home, we were generally stoned out of our ever-loving minds. It's a miracle we all survived. Some of our classmates were not so lucky. Car wrecks sadly took the lives of some local teens driving to and from the beach.

Out of the open window in the back seat, I gave a thumbs up to the oncoming vehicles with boards on top. Our surf reports at the time came from other surfers. When we saw a vehicle with boards, other surfers would put hands out of the window and flip your wrist to thumbs-up and thumbs-down positions to get a response. The west-bound surfers leaving the beach, signaled a thumbs-up if the waves were sizable and ridable, and on less lucky days a thumbs-down.

I later thought about my kneejerk threat to quit surfing. With surfing you're really into it or you're not. You are in or out. You are a surfer, which means for life, or you're not. In my reality, I couldn't quit. I am a surfer, meaning I will always surf. Surfing is one of those spiritual-like sports that can't easily be replaced. In the surf culture, there's a solid bond between surfers. It's an individual sport enjoyed ideally in a group. It embodies the element of surprise which could result in either euphoria or extreme risk dealing with nature with inherent dangerous situations. Therefore, surfing buddies watch out for each other. After a bad wipe out or shark encounter, surfers don't let their friends sit on the beach for long. They find a way to get the rattled surfer to try again. I would always paddle back out, whether it was surfing after a scare or any situation that presented an obstacle. Life is full of fear. Life is full of unpredictable shit. You don't give up what is important to you. You don't let scares and snafus stifle you. Grab your board. Get your head back together. Put it in your past. There is no alternative, but to paddle back out.

CHAPTER 16, COIN-TOSS COLLEGE

I was readying to graduate from Foggy Lake High School in spring in the late 1970s. I earned good, but not great grades. I masked my growing substance abuse issues with being a good student, participating in sports, and maintaining continual employment. My peers and parents believed everything with me was just fine as a normal high school senior.

I was warm to the idea of college but not hot. I wanted to work, surf, party and not commit to anything. My dad thought otherwise. A few months earlier, he had prepared applications for me for the University of Florida and Florida State University. My dad had no education, was a decorated World War II veteran and a no-nonsense kind of man. I was a little afraid of him, so I was going to college. In those days we did things that our parents said we were to do. Their logic was simply, "... because I told you so." We didn't argue anyway. Parents were respected and the fathers generally were the true head of households and disciplinarians.

The acceptance letters came in from both colleges on the same day. My Pop asked, "Which school do you want to go to?"

My interest level was low. It was a ho-hum coin-toss question for me. Apathetically I asked, "Which one is the Gators?"

He said, "University of Florida in Gainesville."

The word "Gainesville" sounded good and conjured up images of rock concerts, drugs and pretty girls.

I said, "I'll go to that one."

This is the late 1970s, not current day, so I could get college acceptance with a 3.4 GPA. At the time, if a student could pay for college tuition, books and housing, they could likely get accepted into some college as a B-grade student. A few decades later, it became much harder to get into the state schools because more people were attending so there was less spaces for students. I was 18 and headed to Gainesville to be a Gator after I finished high school and the post-high school graduation parties. My indifferent college commitment was about to be a landmark decision in my life.

CHAPTER 17, GRAD WEEK IN NEW SMYRNA BEACH

In June, we were set to walk and get our diplomas from Foggy Lake High School. The school held the graduation ceremony on the uneven sand and weed football field. It was brutally hot and muggy. In current day Central Florida, seniors walk to get their diplomas in the cool comfort of the Amway Center in Orlando or the Arena at University of Central Florida. These venues were not yet created in the late 1970s.

Weasel D, The Rat and I did some bong hits with The Boxer so named because he got in fights in high school, and Leisureman a friend so named because he managed to stay under-employed. We met before our graduation ceremony at Sweetwater Pines at the park on a lake with a boat ramp, dock, picnic tables and such. Once high, we drove together to the school to get our diplomas. As mentioned, the temperature was boiling. We were all spread out in alphabetical order by our last names among the hundreds of graduates standing in the heat. We were sweating profusely under our polyester graduation gowns, accelerated by our prior night's consumption of Lowenbrau and Columbian Gold. After moving the cap tassel to the opposite side and the tossing of the graduation caps, taking of photos, and ripping off of the graduation gowns, it was on.

The rite-of-passage in Central Florida for graduating from high school was Grad Week at New Smyrna Beach. The day after high school graduation, my gang and I were in the thick of the activity. Most other kids from my high school, and all the teenagers of all ages not just graduates, from all of the other local high schools, also caravanned to the beach. It was one big surf fest and beach party.

The Poodle, Weasel D and I had saved and saved to have funds for our week of frolic. We all delivered pizzas, did landscaping, worked at restaurants and other part time jobs. With our earnings, we booked a two-bedroom condo at Hacienda Del Sol. There weren't many hotels in New Smyrna, but some owners rented condos and small Florida ranch style houses.

Beach Week was what you would expect of 18-year-olds. It was chock full of chasing members of the opposite sex, usually unsuccessfully. The agenda was getting stoned at every opportunity, drinking beer and other alcoholic beverages, and surfing whenever we could find a peak forming up on the horizon. As Florida surfers, we had to work pretty hard to find our waves. Luckily a little surf swell came in mid-week so we paddled out right in front of our rented condo for playful chest to head high surf. The other days, we drove north on the beach to the inlet or south to Bethune Beach to find waves. That week set off a high-energy momentum of socializing and surfing and the whole summer was a celebration of youth.

As the summer was ending, we were all finishing our part time jobs and preparing to leave our Sweetwater life. In the yearbook some girls noted things like, "I wish I had known you better and we had gone out. Let's stay in touch." No matter how much people say they will stay in touch, in the days of landline telephones and writing letters on paper to mail, the likelihood of staying in touch was slim. Between the preparations for college and massive partying, I had moments of melancholia as I knew I was closing my chapter of childhood. Luckily for me, I would bring much of my childhood, preferred people and activities right into my dorm room and beyond.

CHAPTER 18, THE ACADEMICS OF UF LIFE

The blissful summer-long party and surf session before college was ending. The first week of September, I loaded my gold 1968 VW Bug affectionately known as The Golden Bud referring to Columbian Gold reefer, the strongest bud available at that time. I lived for it. I pointed The Golden Bud north on U.S. Route 441 towards Gainesville. In the driveway of my parents' home, my mom was sobbing. My dad was stoic. Reading their emotions, I realized my life was about to change dramatically. I was leaving home for the first time and entering adulthood.

The two-hour drive passed quickly after a toke with "Stairway to Heaven" rocking at top volume. The campus was abuzz. What a beautiful sight! Some 30,000 students were converging and descending upon this little college town. It was a pleasant and startling surprise to me to see the sheer number and diversity of students.

I was assigned to Broward Hall, a small dorm room for three males. I arrived just three days before the start of classes. There was nowhere close to park to the dorm, so I was relegated to carrying a stereo, my clothes, my surfboard and my few possessions almost a half mile from the parking lot near 441.

In the dorm, the best beds and the closet space had been commandeered. One roommate was a future physician from New York City, who would later die of aids. He was a clean-cut amicable guy with the appearance through our eye contact that he was ready to party. His folks who were helping him settle in seemed to have a different idea for his college experience and eyed me suspiciously. It might have been the odor of marijuana, my shoulder length long hair, my surfboard, or the Led Zeppelin albums. Most parents were there. It was unusual to go by myself as a freshman. It was a rite of passage for my dad to make me figure out college on my own. I had no idea what to expect. I had only visited the campus one time. This was before the internet so I didn't preview anything online. Doc's parents were there and guided me towards Tigert Hall where I was to sign up for classes.

I headed to Gainesville my freshman year with more questions than answers about my future. While I had grades good enough to get into UF, I was not a scholar. That became even more clear when my first report card showed a 2.3 GPA. I was surprised because I studied and tried. As my freshman year evolved, I studied more and sat in the front of the classrooms. To get my grades up, I picked the easiest classes. By the end of my freshman year, my last report card gleamed with a 4.0. I ruled out some options for my education and career path during that year. I couldn't pass accounting to get into business school. One down. I was kicked to the curb in a journalism class. He didn't like the way I wrote. For an advertising class assignment, I wrote a headline about smiling eyes for an eye doctor. The professor made fun of my idea. The girls in the class afterwards affirmed that he was unusually hard on me and my ideas. Two down. Now, political science classes, they just clicked.

I settled into a routine of picking classes given by the same professors. They were fascinating people. They had remarkable lives and had dedicated themselves to passing on their knowledge to us Political Science majors. I randomly signed up for a class called Politics in Developing Nations. I fell into the company of Professor Rene who was of communist persuasion. French was his first language and his lectures were difficult to understand. He was a political scientist born in the 1930s. He was out there. I was in the front row drinking in his lectures. I was also smelling his body odor and halitosis as he was European without the same hygiene habits as us American students. I had a front row seat to the world through this man, and his language and cultural differences were part of that education. His class was sparsely attended because college kids weren't interested in developing nations in the late 1970s. I didn't even know what countries he was referring to in some of the lectures. I viewed this guy as so knowledgeable about the world. I was young and wanted an A grade. He gave me the A and also a lot of big world vision of concepts I had not before considered. He made us think. He would go into the details of violence in Central Africa. He would start talking and stare out of the window like he was going back in time and sharing real live history with us. He would tell us, "Rwanda was intimidating for me, not like you sissies sitting here in your safe comfortable Florida life." In his crumpled untucked shirt, he would talk about his real-life boots on the ground escapades in African countries where he was involved in setting up some kind of government. He told us he was arrested for his political activities trying to help these countries.

From the professor's viewpoint, he was partially of the opinion that capitalism can result in people being preyed upon and kept down while others prosper on the backs of the disenfranchised. I was alarmed that someone would stand up and intimate that the U.S. of A. was not the most amazing and powerful country in the universe. How could he challenge capitalism, especially teaching on U.S. soil? He was not afraid to teach different points of view including possible benefits of socialist nations. I didn't always agree with him. I'm not communist. I just remember thinking it was so edgy and interesting that he was willing to speak out. He radically and positively influenced my interests and my direction in college. I had been floating around and this guy made me think. There was a big world out there and he was introducing me to it one lecture at a time.

I engaged with many acclaimed academics who molded my career and adult life. While Professor Rene traveled the world, Professor Crews wrote about it. I would see him drinking at Lillian's and didn't realize what a badass he was until I took one of his literature classes. It was pure serendipity; I was looking at part of my future self. He was an alcoholic, coke head and novelist obsessed with cock fighting and dog fighting. In his class, he sliced and diced my writing but he didn't fail me. I was completely mesmerized by his lectures.

What I really learned from these professors was that it was acceptable to have a different opinion, path, or way of life than the mainstream. I was different and would continue to be different, just like Professor Rene and Professor Crews.

CHAPTER 19, SATURDAYS SURFING OR ON THE FIELD OF SCREAMS

The professors, the friends, the girls, the whole phenomenon of college made me fall in love with university life in the late 1970s and early 1980s. I developed a deep and enthusiastic allegiance to my institution. I grew a deep love for University of Florida. Love meaning to nurture, pay close attention to, and defend the reputation of it at all costs. Within short order on the campus, I was bleeding orange and blue. Just like the students who are committed to garnet and gold, or maze and blue, or big orange, or scarlet and silver, or black and gold, I was true to my team's colors.

My affinity grew quickly and strongly to UF. I would stroll the campus by 7 a.m. weekdays. I discovered the wonders of the drug caffeine during one of these strolls in the General Purposes Building A, or G.P.A. The building housed six classrooms, where tenured professors gave lectures all day. Coffee at the G.P.A. was ten cents a cup. Being the predictive addictive type, I would get pissed off and flustered for my day on the rare occasions when the coffee machine did not work. Most days started well with my dime cup of kick-start. Misty foggy mornings on this north Florida campus were spent quietly reviewing books and notes outdoors waiting for the wonderous campus to come alive. Sitting there, every brick of the university soaked into me. I was apprehensive to go to Gainesville and now I couldn't get enough of college life.

Then came the first football weekend. I had zero understanding of the passion, and passion is not a strong enough word for the college football fan zealots. Within weeks I was one of them, the obnoxious UF fans. Football on Florida Field is not just a social event to watch a football game, but instead it morphed into an outlet for loud and outrageous debauchery. The tribalistic mantra of "We are wonderful and they suck" pervaded every game regardless of the opposing team. Tickets were near-free to students in those days. Since I was stoned on a lot on my off hours, I was the last to sign up for the ultra-cheap tickets. As a result, I got seats in the most remote corner of the student side of Florida Field. In the fall of my first year, the Gators win-loss record was four and nine by year's end. In my second year they won zero games. I was hooked regardless of their win record. During the first two fall seasons, my friends and I happily bounced to Florida Field for the carnage. Bolstered by beer, Jack

Daniel's and other chemicals, we would don our brightest Gator gear and then go scream and cheer until hoarse for our esteemed team.

With each team song learned, with each new game day tradition, and other jackass-ery, I enthusiastically transformed into a rabid Gator fan. I felt like no other place in the universe existed quite like Saturdays in Gainesville. Long-legged tan girls wore skimpy Dolphin brand shorts and tight braless Gator T-shirts. They screamed and bounced around when Mr. Two Bits, Albert the Alligator mascot, or the other characters came by to raise the cheering volume. The student section view was almost too much for a testosterone-filled 18-year-old male to handle. While Ole Miss and some of the other southern schools in the Southeastern Conference wore business suit attire to football games, the kickoff attire in tropical weather for this school and this generation, was all blue, orange, cotton, tight and small.

The screaming and shenanigans were entertaining. Students brought in blow up sex dolls, inflated them, dressed them in the opposing team's colors, then passed the dolls from the front row up to the top of the bleachers row by row. After the doll was passed 75-yards up to the last row, the air-filled doll was hoisted over the stadium wall much to the insane delight of all in attendance.

Before all the deep security nonsense, we would leave the stadium and come back at will. Students left at halftime to plug themselves with more alcohol or whatever and come back to watch the game. During my freshman year, my roommate Doc plied himself too much with Jack Daniel's. He went to the restroom during the fourth quarter and passed out in a stall. He woke up three hours later to a completely empty stadium. He was bewildered but safe when he made his way back to our dorm with the story of his blackout. We dorm-mates laughed at him hysterically for days. It was a safer time on college campuses. If your friend went missing for a few hours, you assumed he was on an adventure, not abducted.

The teams are different now, too. In the past, football players were recruited from the student body. Now many are hired assassins, kids from the hood, who have low grades if they even attend classes. In Gainesville, and other college towns with a football program in present day, a fraud is perpetrated in the form of college football season. Young men who for the most part would never have been admitted to UF or other major universities with their high school transcripts, are now donning their team's colors as they take to the field to play football. College football is a giant business. Kids are being recruited younger and younger by college football coaches. Long gone are the days when the football players were picked from the students attending the universities on academic merit. College athletics felt personal when I was in college. The student population was smaller and the rules were stricter about college athletes actually attending classes. So, routinely we'd be in classes with the football players and became friends with them. We all studied together and helped each other with homework and we felt aligned as fellow students. The current culture feels much different. The kids recruited to play football at major universities today are hired guns lured to these schools not for the love of the game, or the institution, but for the big shot of going pro someday. It appears that attending classes and mingling with peers is an after-thought at best for them. The kids playing now aren't a part of the us in the us-versus-them psyche of college football. Players don't give a shit about the fans, or the schools. It's just a theatre to show their skills to go pro. It's a societal flaw, not a flaw of the players.

Whatever the case, be it the fellow students of my heyday or the hired guns of today, when I walk into that stadium on a football Saturday with family members, or old friends, spiritual-like chills take over my body and my being. Tears well up when I hear the band crank up one of the UF fight songs. The misty eyes are from recalling fondly the misty mornings walking in the dew on campus.

On game days while I was in college, if there were waves on the coast, we surfed early then attended the games in the afternoons. We surfed often. Gainesville as a geographic phenomenon had plenty of fun within close proximity. It was just a little over an hour drive east to St. Augustine, the oldest city in the U.S. and a popular surf spot. It was a cool drive through the country through little cities with historical character like Interlachen, Keystone Heights and Palatka. Once we got to St. Augustine in the pre-dawn hours, we could see the sun rise over the Atlantic Ocean as we paddled out in surf spots like Blow-Hole or Middles. In St. Augustine, we could also drive on the beach, just like in New Smyrna Beach. Driving on the beach always had the makings of lots of shenanigans to go with it. In the 1970s through the 1980s there was not a whole lot of law around to try to cool off various kinds of fun. In other words, we could surf in the morning, fire up a grill at 11 a.m., and suck down all the beer and rum we wanted without much concern about the po-po snooping around to make a cheap bust.

After an east coast sunrise surfing session, or after UF games, if we had the gumption, we rolled across the state 60 minutes to the west of Gainesville, to Cedar Key. There we consumed the freshest of seafood at places like The Captain's Table and watched the sun sink into the Gulf of Mexico on the same day that we saw it rise over the Atlantic. We had those kinds of days scientifically timed so we could take in everything that North Central Florida had to offer. We mastered the surfing and sipping synchronicity.

My high school friend The Boxer also was a Gator. Along with some other surfer athletes we started the National Scholastic Surfing Association or NSSA chapter on the UF campus which is still active decades later. The Boxer was the first president and I was the first treasurer. We got the funding from the university and prepared all of the paperwork to start the campus club. We had surf contests on weekends in St. Augustine, New Smyrna Beach, Canaveral National Seashore, Cocoa Beach, Sebastian Inlet and other spots along Florida's east coast. We competed against other newly formed teams at Florida State University, University of Central Florida, University of Miami and Flagler College. Some of the members of the various teams planned surf trips to the Bahamas for spring breaks. It was great fun to surf in different spots and have friendly competition with other surfers. We tried to schedule the surf contests so the surfers wouldn't miss big football games or the homecoming games at the various colleges.

Saturdays, and every day of Gator college life, suited this surfer student just fine.

CHAPTER 20, THE LAW SCHOOL LIGHTBULB

By my junior year, my grades were bumping around 3.8 to 4.0 GPA. A degree in Political Science by itself did not seem marketable. I could always teach as a backup profession, but I wanted a career choice with more action and income potential. I ruled out earning a living with my hands, or with sales. I wanted something heavy on talking and writing with a large measure of independence. I talked to family and friends and the campus career counselors and I had zip of a plan for what to do after college. As my senior year approached, I was getting mildly panicky.

I was a lone wolf having coffee at General Purposes Building A. I bumped into an attractive gal who was in some of the same classes. We started at UF at the same time and were on the same flight plan. She was from Ft. Lauderdale and had a twin sister with the same beachy look. We called them H-one and H-two for Hottie one and two. I was loosely acquainted with her from frequenting GPA and the same bars and restaurants. We were close enough to give friendly observations and advice.

She asked what everyone was asking, "What are you doing after you graduate?"

I admitted to her that I did not know.

She responded, "You don't strike me as a company man. Have you thought about law school?"

It had never crossed my mind. At the heart of it all, I'm very insecure. Neither my dad nor anybody else ever bolstered me, showed confidence in me, or gave praise for my efforts. So, I was not brimming with confidence as a young man.

H-one stopped me in my tracks. She was worldly and knew what it took to be a lawyer and she suggested I could do it. This co-ed acquaintance believed in me and saw what I didn't see in myself. I wasn't confident enough in myself to even think that goal was reachable. It seemed like an impossible idea at first glance. She told me it was not impossible, but a simple idea. All I had to do was have a good GPA and take the Law School Admissions Test or LSAT. I couldn't believe that was all there was to it. Just that simple nudging lit the lightbulb. Based on one light conversation with a pretty girl and my life had direction. Ten minutes prior, I had no idea what I would do for a career. Like many pivotal points in my life, the decision struck with lightning speed and launched me towards my destiny. I was going to be a lawyer. Decision was made.

For the rest of my adult life, as with every attorney, I answer the question, "Why lawyer?" with the answer, "A short casual conversation clicked on the lightbulb."

I started researching law school. I needed to take the Stanley Kaplan LSAT course, so I promptly raised the money to sign up for the course. How did I pay for the course? Well, I sold a stock of dope.

For ten weekends, I took the course in downtown Gainesville in a musty building Stanley Kaplan rented. I sat for the law school admissions test on the appointed day and ended up in the top 10%. It was an aptitude test for practical judgment and logical reasoning. It was different than the Florida Bar Exam, which you do have to study prior to taking.

My index score was in place, my acceptable GPA and law school admissions test was completed. Being ever single-minded, I applied to one law school and one law school only, University of Florida.

My application was denied. I was mortified. People with lower LSAT scores were admitted, but I was denied.

I made an appointment with the dean of the law school and asked why I blew these people away with my test score and they got accepted and I didn't.

He looked at my transcripts, records and personal statements. He pompously looked across his mahogany desk, lowered his reading glasses and looked me in the eyes. He bluntly pointed out the reason I didn't get in was there were no fireworks in the application. His thumb tapped my thin application after he flipped through the pages without reading a word. I couldn't muster the courage to ask what fireworks meant. If I was worthy of law school admission, I must be expected to know what fireworks meant. I had a lightbulb and now I needed fireworks.

I limped back to my parents' home for the summer before my senior year. I decided that fireworks meant connections. I arranged to work at the biggest firm in Orlando at the time, which I jokingly called Billings, Pompous and Tackiton. The partners, without knowing me at all, had their secretaries generate the canned letter of recommendation to their alma maters. The translation of the canned letter is, "I send lots of donor money so let this kid that I don't know into the damn school." Fireworks ... boom!

I made applications to law schools at University of Florida again, Florida

State, University of Miami and Stetson University. I had much better luck with the fireworks attached to the applications. I was granted admission to all of them with my fireworks show.

As law school approached, not only was I peddling dope but also holding down three jobs in Central Florida.

I showed up at 5 a.m. at the local Country Club every day to clean, water and prepare the clay tennis courts for the muckety-mucks who were going to play tennis.

From there I would blow into downtown Orlando to pick up two giant duffle bags of daily mail for the law firm. I schlepped them into their office in a high rise building on Orange Avenue. I would begin my day at the law firm as a runner and a clerk.

On most days, I would leave the law firm, freshen up at home, then check into my third job as a doorman at a popular bar and restaurant in the Altamonte Mall. Rather than a doorman, I preferred to think of myself as a bouncer. It was a happening bar scene at the time and I was responsible for checking out all the pretty girls waiting in the long lines to get entrance. I multi-tasked and would leave pre-orders of coke for trusted friends in my unlocked car in the parking lot. I would place the orders in designated hiding places such as under a particular floor mat, in the center console or in the glove compartment.

I always had an entrepreneurial spirit so I planned ahead for many sales. One time at UF, I left a gram hidden at The Boxer's room at his frat house when they bought one. Sure enough, the call came at midnight for a second one and I directed him to the hiding place. He looked like a magician to his friends that night. I had a sixth-sense for planning ahead for sales that served me well through the years whether it was selling little bags of product or later fees for my legal services.

I was starting to tell people I was going to law school and I was getting more positive attention than normal. People I did not know well were starting to cozy up to me. The girls especially seemed to like the notion of me practicing law. The perception of the me in the world was evolving now that I was headed to law school. People can be funny that way.

CHAPTER 21, THE LAW OF ATTRACTION

The Gator era continued as I entered the University of Florida College of Law in the early 1980s. My academic credentials were not strong enough to get in the fall semester, so I started in January. I was granted admission with 200 other hopeful would-be lawyers. Where college had come easily once I got in the school of Political Science, the study of law was stunningly difficult. I did not naturally take to it at all.

In preparation to attend law school, I tried to ditch the surfer look. I cut my hair short and bought a few pairs of khakis, a pair of classic Oxford leather shoes and a Members Only jacket. As I proudly donned this ensemble on the first day of law school, one of my new classmates who had been on the UF surf team with me heckled loudly from the second floor of the law school pavilion, "Well, don't you look like the law school nerd?" He laughed hysterically at my smart lawyer style. He took no measure to try to fit in with our more conservative classmates. In law school the first year was exceedingly competitive and cut-throat. Students were vying for high grades, membership in the law review and moot court. There were only so many spaces in each of these programs and we were competing fiercely. I started competing for favor with the professors with my first impression, my wardrobe. Dressing appropriately and respectfully would be a tip I would later give my clients for court appearances.

First year law students, or One-Ls as we were referred to, quickly sized each other up and formed study groups. Study groups had meeting times where students compared and shared notes, discussed reading material, guessed what might comprise the final exam, and decided what material would be paramount to study. This was especially daunting because law school only had one exam per semester. The GPA and ranking of each student at the college of law rested on one end of semester exam. It was a lingering monster that you had to wait for months to confront.

After the anguish of attacking the monster exam, the grades were mailed to us. When we returned to class, there were students with grand smug smiles and you knew they had crushed it. There were those who acted nonchalant who did fairly well. Then those at my grade level, felt ashamed and looked at the ground. I processed in my mind the results of my first semester, one B and the rest Cs and Ds. I couldn't believe it. I deflated into a mental tailspin. I had indeed studied my ass off, joined a study group and gave my best effort. I figured there had to be some sort of mistake. In my mind, I had understood the questions posed by the law professors that required essay responses. I had certainly responded with logic and brilliance. Could they not read my handwriting? We wrote in cursive on paper before laptops were commonly used in education.

I made an appointment to see the professors. In each of the isolated offices I was greeted with little interest on the part of my mentors. UF was considered the top law school in the state if not the whole South at the time. The school hired professors not because they were acclaimed attorneys, but because they were renowned authors and speakers that commanded attention and money without actually practicing law. None of the professors who were willing to see me would go into detail where I had floundered on exams. They all generally suggested that I focus on spotting the most important and prominent issues from the questions and perhaps not give such verbose responses. It brought back mental images of journalism classes where my writing style was also underappreciated. I was determined to uncover the secret for excelling in the exams but I needed specific direction. I left these meetings with less of an idea as to how to be a top-notch law student than when I had entered their comfortable den-like offices.

I ended my first year of law school in the top 95% of my class; which means the bottom 5. It was a conundrum. I studied hard, participated, and attended every class.

My peers told me I did well when the professors used the Socratic System. The law school teaching method was based on how the Greek Philosopher Socrates taught his students by asking questions and generating debate to imbue critical thinking. So, I mastered a fourth century B.C. communication technique, but I still needed to translate that skill to current day law school grades. Professors picked students' names from a seating chart of the class and engaged in back and forth banter.

During one particularly contentious back and forth, a popular professor asked at the end of a colloquy, "Mr. Wander your line of thinking as to whether or not there was a contractual relationship between the parties is not valid. Do you know why that is?"

My response was, after a pause, "Because you are in charge here and you disagree with my answers."

The class of a hundred students burst out in raucous laughter. The professor raised his forefinger to the class to regain order. He looked around the room with his forefinger still in the air.

He spoke, "Mr. Wander is absolutely correct. This is how the law works and really how the world works. You must know thy judge."

So, while my answer had not contained complex nuances of contractual negotiations, it was perceived as a powerful insight by this professor. When the class ended and students filed out from the classroom, the professor, of whom I was very intimidated, placed his hand on my shoulder, and said, "You're going to do well in law. You seem to have an instinct for it so go ahead and follow your path." The professors did not typically dole out compliments to students. I believe he could sense my insecurity and chose to bolster my confidence. It worked. I still remember his encouraging comment to this day. One positive well-worded, well-placed sentence in a human's life can make a difference.

At the end of the second year of law school, I was still making C and D grades despite my earnest efforts. While I was smart enough and focused enough, I could not crack the code to get my first A or a second B.

During this part of career preparation, people around me started asking what part of the law I intended to pursue. My rote response was property law. I had no idea what property law entailed but the answer satisfied the askers.

At this point in the second year, law school students started looking for summer internships and clerkships. Those in the top 10% of the class, or members of the law review or moot court, were granted interviews for summer clerkships at blue chip firms and big-name firms. The prime spots paid between $800 to $1000-per-week which was a fortune to a financially struggling law student. Students of sufficient caliber and pedigree were invited to interview on campus and had a pick of their firm and city and gleefully informed the rest of us of their grand offers and pending successes. I only knew about the interviews and subjects of them as told by my friends with better grades. My method of finding a clerkship was more basic. There was a bulletin board in the common area of the law school which posted typewritten job openings on index cards for job opportunities. The cards gave a job description and told where to mail a resume and cover letter. One index card stood out. It read, "Part-time summer internship in downtown Orlando, Criminal Defense and Personal Injury, Contact the Law Office of Andrew Pepperdine." I mailed my cover letter and resume and somehow avoided the topic of my grades. I informed the potential employer I could meet anytime in Orlando for an interview.

In May, I met Andy, as I would call my summer boss, at a restaurant in Altamonte Springs called, aptly enough, The Smugglers Inn. Although I had been the only applicant for the job, he told me he would consider employing me as his clerk and would get back with me.

I really, really wanted this job. After all, it was part-time. This notion smacked of plenty of extracurricular activities including golf, surfing and drinking. My dad would be happy that I had a job. I didn't need the money because I was still moving dope. Part-time was a perfect fit.

The next day a voicemail was left on a scratchy Panasonic answering machine at my folks' house in Sweetwater Pines. It was Andy's assistant informing me that he would extend me an offer and to call back. To not seem too anxious, I waited two hours to return the call. I sealed the deal. I was to start my legal career June 1. My rate of pay was $12-per-hour. I could not have been more ecstatic. My new mentor was young, passionate about law, and was accessible to tutor me because he was a sole practitioner.

On my first day on the job, he told me to familiarize myself with several files of criminal cases. I did as he asked and found the content of the files compelling. Then came the assignment. He told me to research and write motions, backed up by Florida case law precedent, to request the court to throw evidence out in these cases. I don't believe my facial expression betrayed me. I had no idea what he was saying. The criminal law classes and constitutional law classes were all theory and the case law used was ancient. Most troubling was that I didn't even know what a motion was. So, I got up my courage and walked into his office and fessed up to my lack of experience. I needed direction. I asked if there was some sort of guidebook or rule book that would list motions for me and how to write them. He was kind enough to stifle his laugh but smiled broadly. He clasped his hands behind his head and said, "OK, Clerk-breath close that door behind you and we have some talking to do." Clerk-breath would become another unfortunate nickname for me thanks to my new adviser.

Andy explained you could file a motion for anything. He explained in this context he wanted to file motions about the police behavior in these cases and examine if the behavior was proper under Florida law. He provided me with motions he had used in previous cases to get the notion of what he expected. Before that day, I did not fully comprehend the direct personal impact of our Constitution on the lives of everyday people. Once I actually sat before his clients and listened to their predicaments and how these criminal charges affected them, in real life in real time, I was certain of my calling in this life.

I spent that summer following him around the court and watched him argue real cases with real law in front of real judges and real juries with real consequences for very real clients. By virtue of poor grades, landing this pitiful low paying job, and this very serendipitous rapport with young Andy, I knew I was on a collision course to be a street level criminal defense lawyer. It worked. It fit. It made sense.

I had been hassled on a number of occasions by very aggressive cops, yet not arrested. I wondered how in the hell they got away with some of the things they did to citizens. Since I had not been arrested, I never got to see how the story ended for people who were prosecuted. This was all starting to fit like a glove in three short months.

Andy's eyes would light up, not just at my youthful enthusiasm for his vocation, but also the stream of clients I generated. My pot smoking, coke snorting, bar brawling buddies started to line up at his door to hire him for his legal services. He was throwing me pretty good bonuses along the way as a thank you for his bump in business.

So, while I was glibly bouncing the streets of downtown Orlando, working with this solo practitioner lawyer, I was bumping into my high-achiever classmates who were clerking for the blue-blood firms of Orange County. While I was happy with my summer clerkship, they were utterly miserable. The firms were working them north of 50 hours a week, indoctrinating them to the concept of billable hours, and generally working them into the ground. Worse yet, most of their free time was spoken for as well. There were firm functions which were boring beyond description and voluntary work meetings on weekends, which weren't voluntary at all. It was insane that these guys were running up and down the law firm hallways trying to impress the firm partners. The brightest and clearest direction from above was that I was not to be a suit-wearing stuffy company man in the field of law. I was to be a criminal defense guy in the trenches. Thank the Lord above for inferior grades. When Andy and I parted ways after that summer, he said I could come back and work full-time anytime.

He encouraged me that I would have many, many options once I was sworn into The Florida Bar.

As a natural consequence, when I returned to Gainesville, my grades skyrocketed. After being an apprentice in the actual field, seeing actual human drama full of the spirit of the law and truly learning about it, I was unafraid to voice my opinion. This newfound confidence transitioned into law school exams as well. I was more readily spotting red hot legal issues and giving more on-target answers. The law school professors noticed and rewarded me with an intangible respect and significantly better grades.

Law school is not a trade school. It doesn't teach you how to practice law. The serendipitous experience over the summer taught me how to practice law. It's one thing to hear about law in a classroom and another to actually learn it. It's like you can watch a video on how to surf till the cows come home and still not be able to paddle out to the lineup. You can watch the step-by-step video over and over again and think surfing looks easy, but until you participate and get in the water on a board, you don't know how to surf.

The more I learned about criminal defense, the more it clicked in my brain. I knew it was for me.

People asked why I chose criminal defense and told me there was no money in it. It's a well kept secret that it's lucrative. Everyone around me assumed that lawbreakers and eventual defendants couldn't possibly afford to pay fees enough to provide an upscale lifestyle for a young lawyer. My law school peers and bigwigs from the blue stocking firms felt the same way. I would learn in time that they were wrong.

People looked down their nose at lawyers for choosing criminal defense; it's a thing. My classmates who were pursuing more conventional paths in traditional law firms would give me a quick blank stare then catch themselves. They would remark something innocuous like, "Oh, that sounds interesting." What they were really thinking was what a nasty sad state it would be to go through seven years of college just to represent dirtbag after dirtbag and probably not get paid. Most of the lawyers who later ended up in criminal defense arrived there because their resume only earned employment with the prosecutor's office or public defender's office. Most claimed they chose those positions to get trial experience as quickly as possible out of law school. The truth was most of them accepted these low paying disrespected positions because they were the only offers they received. The new public defenders were viewed as lowly. The district attorneys had slightly better pay and were viewed more favorably because their outward job description was to put bad guys behind bars.

In later years, whenever someone pointed out that I was a criminal lawyer, I winced internally. That sounded like Jack is a criminal and Jack is a lawyer. Depending upon the circumstances, I corrected them and added a word ... "I'm a criminal defense lawyer." The term criminal lawyer has a bad ring to it like a punchline in a lawyer joke.

There might be more prestigious areas of the law, but for me, my interest level was and still is high in crime and punishment.

CHAPTER 22, OMENS OF CRIMINAL DEFENSE

My interest in practicing criminal defense evolved from my clerkship with Andy, and was amplified by my contacts with police during my somewhat reckless youth. Not only did I have omens for me becoming a boozer, but also for my choice of higher education and my inevitable career choice. Fate gave me some light brushes with the law by almost getting popped for weed and coke a few times. These experiences would give me genuine compassion for my clients in the future.

In the spring of 1978, Weasel D and I were eyeballing high school graduation. About sunset, we were rolling along in Weasel D's The Green Machine eastbound on the then quiet State Road 436 in Altamonte Springs with the destination of Sam's Woodshed Pub. We were going to see a local band of some renown SOMF City. SOMF was an acronym for Sit On My Face band. When family members of the band were in attendance at gigs, the band would claim the initials stood for Sons Of Maitland, Florida.

We were in a party mood listening to music, making plans for summer surf trips, and smoking weed. To smoke all the way down to the end of a hand-rolled cigarette looking joint, we used a hemostat. Roach clips were popular, too, but a metal medical surgical tool with scissor like handles with a small precision grip at the end was perfect for grasping our just-about-gone joints. The sticky resin built up at the end of the grip and a small piece of paper from the joint was stuck. So, Weasel D put it out of the window to shake it and flick off the paper. The wind caught the fire and it lit up like a sparkler. This caught the attention of Altamonte Springs' finest. Here came the blue lights. We had broken no traffic laws. We were clean except the new bag. Columbian Gold bags were about three-inches before the more potent and seedless Sensimilla bags would come on the scene at just one-inch and therefore easier to conceal. So, off went the pickup to the side of the road and down went the new bag stuffed down my pants on top of my cock. Weasel D got aggressive and demanded, "Why did you pull me over? I didn't do anything." The more experienced cop took ahold of Weasel D. Asking no questions, the mature officer took Weasel D by the collar and put him by the truck. The less experienced cop calmly asked me to get out of the truck and gingerly gave me a cursory search. The other cop had Weasel D and was giving him a more comprehensive search as loudmouth Weasel D taunted him, "I'm not getting off on that shit." The duo didn't find the weed even though we reeked and put on a fireworks display. Reluctantly they let us go free. They had no reason to charge us with any traffic violations or crimes.

Back in the truck, we were mesmerized. They wouldn't tell us why they stopped us and we were complying with the rules of traffic. We had this deep feeling of being wronged and that something should be done about it. As punk-ass kids, we thought we should call their supervisors so we could teach them a lesson. We were 18 and looked 15 and just about always stoned to the bone. We had a near miss, but alas, all was good so we went along with our plan to see our favorite band.

SOMF City was so precise in playing cover tunes that they sometimes sounded better than the real bands. They covered Led Zeppelin, Queen, Lynyrd Skynyrd, Jackson Browne and many other popular 1970s bands. That night they kicked in the first set when we walked in the bar with the song "Free Bird." We were in fact free as birds. We were damn lucky to be free.

A few years later while attending UF, my friends and I were becoming regulars in the bar scene in Gainesville. One night at Big Daddy's Lamplighter Lounge parking lot, Weasel D, The Boxer and I were sitting in my VW Rabbit. It was a beat-up surf-mobile and at the moment was filled with a cloud of smoke. We heard a knock on the door and saw the flashlight beams of cops. I took the roach and swallowed what could be the evidence. I was OCD about keeping my cars clean. I went over the VW with a fine-toothed comb before we went out so I was certain we only had one joint and it was now gone. So, we were defiant. Then the cops in retaliation were giving us a hard time. The guys were being loud and proud with the cops. Then time stopped and we heard the words, "What is this Mr. Wander?" as one cop held up a vial with a small amount of cocaine residue with a small plastic spoon. Our collective hearts sank as we began back peddling. I thought we were in the clear. I missed one illicit object in an obscure corner of the glove compartment. We upped the ante with the police by being smart and heightened tensions by our brazen stupidity. The cops were not much older than us and not hard-asses once we stopped mouthing off at them. They were somewhat sympathetic, and a little weed or small amount of coke was not a big deal in that era. I jumped into adrenaline filled action with an apology, "Gentlemen, I am so sorry.

We should not have acted this way. We are students and we should know better. I fall on my sword." I pulled out the law school card. I tried everything. Somehow it worked. Cooler heads prevailed and I talked the cops out of the arrests. It became lore in our surf circle and my nickname evolved into The Silver-Tongued Minnow.

Not one to learn my lessons easily, I had a subsequent run-in with the law in Ocala. I was driving at night with a new stash of Sensimilla. I was heading from Orlando to Gainesville in my then piece-of-shit Fiat X19. The car would overheat and stall. I would get stranded often. When this happened, I would wait 90 minutes or so and it would start again. Fiat fiasco car started making the tell-tale noises and I put it in neutral and coasted off to the side of I-75 northbound near an Ocala exit. I pulled out a flashlight and started studying to pass the time. Some 20 minutes later State Troopers pulled up behind me with blue lights flashing. I explained to the two officers about my predicament. They saw I was studying. They asked if I was a student and that seemed to ease any suspicion about me. One of them said, "For your safety I can't leave you here so I'll take you to the Patrol Station in town." This was before cameras were all over the interstates so there was no way I was leaving my valuable cargo in my abandoned car. I thought the ne'er-do-well types along I-75 would break in and steal valuables. I was on the hook for a lot of cash used to buy the pound of Sensimilla. So, the turquoise Adidas duffle bag with the senso wrapped inside surf baggies and t-shirts was going into the trunk of the State Patrol car. I lied and said I made a living with my surfboard, that I was on a surfing scholarship, so they let me take the board from the soft racks on the back of my car and stuff that in the back of their big sedan trunk, too. In the back seat behind the cage I could smell the senso in the trunk. I wondered if they could, too. It was a clash of cultures between me and these marine types. I, however, lived up to my Silver-Tongued Minnow label and did not panic but was polite and compliant.

From the land line at the station, I called the proprietor of the bag, my roommate. I attempted to explain to him that he needed to pick me up in Ocala, like now. He asked reluctantly, "You want me to what? Come get you at the State Trooper Station?" He obviously knew what I was carrying and he was not falling all over himself to get me. He hesitated mightily on the other end of the phone. I was looking around and hoping the marine-types weren't getting suspicious. I calmly asked him a second time to pick me up at the Marion County station because I had car trouble. A very long hour lingered before my roommate nervously eased into the parking lot. I hopped in his truck with the Adidas bag and the surfboard and we drove back to the Fiat on the side of the road which started up right away. Once again, I was free to go. I was again lucky.

My lucky streak continued. From Gainesville, I made trips to South Florida to pick up shit with my surf buddy BB. We would surf our way up the east coast of Florida then dip back to Gainesville. We stopped at the Fort Pierce inlet and the conditions posted on the notice board sign said the surf sucked. We drove a quarter mile then stopped again in front of a sign that said no parking. We wanted to see the lack of surf with our own eyes and look back at the inlet from the dunes. We were jonesing for surf and per usual the rules were not for us. We hopped out of his Z car and ducked over the dunes to get a quick look at the waves. The surf did suck. As we climbed back over the dunes, to our horror we left our doors wide open on both sides. A policeman was hovering. He was within grasp of a stash of coke just sitting on the back floor and five pounds of Columbian in the same Adidas duffle bag I used before. BB was on probation and didn't have a driver's license. He fell into a lot of trouble. He got out of a lot of trouble because his dad was a high-powered attorney in Miami. BB whispered, "Jack, go to the driver's side. You're the driver. Let him talk to you." We were frantic. As I walked towards the open door on the driver's side, the cop said, "Not you, blondie, your friend was driving. I want to talk to him." Now BB's heart was going 5000-beats-a-minute as the cop pointed to him. He was so nervous that he dropped his wallet and his UF student I.D. fell out. The cop picked it up, gave us a look-over, and asked, "You Gators?" I took the cue and explained that we had visited friends in Miami and were on our way back to school for morning classes. We had an amicable exchange about classes and football games. Apparently, before he suited up in uniforms and badges, he also wore blue and orange. He shifted from an adversary to a fellow Gator. The cop's demeanor changed and he said, "I went to Florida, too. Ya'll have a good day." We were idiots just wanting to surf. We were not truly idiots, just lawless. BB was in business school at UF, which at the time was ranked 13th in the U.S. topped only by the Ivy League Schools and I was headed to law school. We picked up some beer and drank our way back to Gainesville commiserating about the near-miss nightmare. We Gators thankfully were heading to Gainesville and not rival FSU in Tallahassee or it could very well have had a different outcome.

The Silver Tongued Minnow would soon leave college life and use similar communication skills to negotiate and sway opinions for favorable outcomes in dealings involving law and order.

CHAPTER 23, THE BARON HALF IN THE BAG

I had a smattering of adventures of all kinds, many with near-misses. Without regard to challenges or consequences, I swung from one thing to another, endured trials and tribulations, overcame the obstacles, and went on to adventure again. My friend Little Mitch graduated from law school about the same time and he called me The Baron from the quirky 1988 film "The Adventures of Baron Munchausen." Law school life and the extended surf safari were over for The Baron. The Virgin Island escape and the subsequent drug running escapades were in my past. My future awaited me. I came back to Florida and passed The Bar.

The late 1980s were on; I can hear the Van Halen music in my head.

I rented an office in the Tinker Building on West Pine Street in downtown Orlando. The 1925 historic structure was named after a baseball player who also built a baseball field for Orlando, Tinker Field. It was a short walk to the courthouse and right in the heart of everything important in my life. I was bubbling all over with gratitude that I could open my own business. I had to pinch myself that my entrepreneurship was reality.

Two practices were in the Pine Street office. The other attorneys were skeptical. I just opened shop. I didn't start at the D.A.'s office or work my way up brown-nosing in a big firm. While never secretive as I should have been about my alcohol and drug use, nobody seemed to know. In my personality, I'm innately driven to be early and return every call. I could appear as though I had it all together. I was tan from my outdoor sports and surfing, and fully immersed in the stream of life. I never missed a beat although I had a ton of shit in my bloodstream.

It was a great advantage to have grown up locally. The first week I opened shop a pot smoker buddy of mine from Cocoa Beach referred a dude from Okeechobee who had been busted in Orlando with 110 pounds of weed. The guy was heavy set, very country and very calm. He informed me in a matter-of-fact fashion that life in Okeechobee was hard and dope smuggling was common in those parts as a way to get by financially in rural Florida. During our initial consultation, I tried to stay cool and act like I had navigated cases like that before. I had not. When the issue of my fee came up, the figure $15,000 randomly popped into my mind and I let it roll off my tongue. He sedately looked at me and said he had to put more change in the parking meter and that he would be right back. I figured he was gone and so was my potential $15,000 fee.

"Shit! Did I quote too much? Did my inexperience show? Was I not on my A-game?" I wondered with great insecurity. After all, I was a little hazy and half in the bag from my cocktails at lunch.

Then miraculously I heard the security doorbell ring and back came the sizable bearded man in the brown plaid shirt and now with a big brown paper bag in his hand. Again, in an unnaturally serene demeanor, like a hunter near a deer, he slowly walked back into my new law office. He set the bag on the desk, it tipped over and cash fell in big chunks on my desk. After we were finished counting $15,000 together, over half the cash he brought in for potential payment was left in the bag.

"Shit!" again I thought.

I could have quoted $100,000 and he would have gladly handed it over to a bright young barrister for his defense. It was a lesson learned about how to charge clients to ask more questions about their finances before setting a fee.

Once we parted company after my assurances that I would defend him to the bitter end, I stacked the cash in my briefcase and cheerfully marched next door to deposit the goods. My intent was to come off as the sleek high-priced defense lawyer to the pretty tellers and bank managers. The bank personnel seemed more curious than impressed. As I was stacking cash on the counter, the sugar-sweet girl-next-door teller from Brooksville, took two steps back and squealed, "That money smells like pot!"

I looked around and calmly asked my blonde banker to please lower her voice. I went immediately from proud and cocky to embarrassed and squeamish. Another lesson learned was not to show off and be boastful.

Many of these attorney – client encounters were to take place at that charming historic Orlando building. Every day was a surprise who might call with legal issues.

CHAPTER 24, A FIRST VICTORY FOR TRUTH, UN MOMENTO DE VERDAD

You couldn't throw a rock in downtown Orlando without hitting a lawyer in the late 1980s when I first opened my firm. The market was rocking but there was and is always room for one more effective lawyer. Most all lawyers, especially criminal defense types, think they are the best. The career is incredibly ego driven. Of course, I'm no different. If I win a jury verdict, I think it's because the way I, and only I, navigated the intricacies of the case in such a way that only I am capable. There has to be some element of ego and confidence to be effective.

The goal is to win. There's no sweeter phrase in the English language to a defense attorney than those words stated from the clerk, "We the jury find the defendant not guilty." I did not hear those words at the conclusion of my first few trials. Since I had not worked for the public defender's office or state attorney's office, I hadn't had formal training in the fine art of jury selection, cross examination, jury instructions or closing arguments.

I was early in my career as a private criminal defense attorney. I was also accepting court appointed cases. These cases were delegated to private criminal defense attorneys because the indigent defendant had a conflict of interest with the public defender's office. So, when the conflict was brought to the judge's attention, they would appoint a private lawyer to defend the client at a rate of $50-per-hour. Defense types typically charge flat fees and aren't practiced at keeping track of billable time, so billing ended up being very liberal.

One of my first appointed cases involved a young defendant Xavier. He was accused of burglarizing cars at a high-end area of town near downtown Orlando known as the Country Club of Orlando. At a glance, evidence seemed strong against Xavier. He was seen in the immediate area of car burglaries shortly after calls to police were made. The cops stopped him briskly walking away from Country Club of Orlando wearing dark clothing, so he generally fit the description of a burglar called in to the police station.

Xavier spoke little English. Spanish was his first language. The arresting officers called a Spanish speaking cop to speak with Xavier in his native language. By the end of the investigation, they had a written confession and he was locked up in the Orange County jail with bond set at $5,000. Xavier was poor and he could not bond out of jail.

I procured the services of a Spanish interpreter, a bubbly rotund Cuban lady, who helped me for decades after this first case. Xavier seemed uneducated and downtrodden but not guilty. He told me as much through the interpreter. He was 23-years-old with no prior contact with the criminal justice system. He had been arrested with $33 in his pocket which he told me he had earned by loading crates of oranges at a packing company on Orange Blossom Trail, not far from the country club. When asked about the confession, he assured me he said no such thing.

Xavier sat in jail for one month before a pre-trial conference before the judge. The prosecuting attorney through interpreter, offered Xavier a deal of probation, community service and no felony conviction. Under normal circumstances, this would not be considered a bad deal. He firmly rejected the offer and the opportunity to leave jail that day. He assured me he wanted a trial. It was a head-scratcher. I thought perhaps he had a psychiatric issue. So, through the Cuban interpreter, I gently told him that with a signed confession I was not sure how I would defend him in front of a jury. He adamantly denied the legitimacy of the signed confession and said his faith would not allow him to plead guilty or no contest to something he did not do. The judge and prosecutor were incensed and agitated that they would have to waste time on a trial where the dude confessed.

I liked Xavier as a person. It was clear that he had a rough upbringing but a good God-given heart. I retreated from the idea of a psychiatric evaluation and dug into the case itself. Then it hit me – I could definitely defend and possibly prevail on the date of the jury trial set two weeks down the road. At the hearing, the prosecutor sweetened the deal to a plea of 60 days in county jail, with credit for time served which was now about 60 days. Xavier refused. The judge called us back in chambers.

The judge said, "Gentlemen, I'm not sure why we are going to trial. The defendant was placed at the scene and signed a confession. What's your defense Mr. Wander?"

I said, "My defense is that he didn't do it. Put your seatbelts on."

This created a murmur of laughter for those present.

Sure enough, the trial started and the civilian witnesses patriotically pointed to my client as the person they saw walking away from the burglarized vehicles. The interpreter dutifully conveyed to Xavier all the goings-on in Spanish. The arresting officer in full uniform solemnly swore that he was the one who obtained the confession from Xavier and thrust the document to the clerk to hand to the jurors so that the nice white jurors could study it.

The confession read, "As I was proceeding northbound on Orange Blossom Trail, I observed two vehicles unoccupied toward the entry of the neighborhood. I tried both vehicle door handles, both were unlocked, and searched the vehicles for any valuables. The first vehicle was a Cadillac blue in color, the second a Volvo white in color. I then proceeded without any items to walk to my home in neighboring Lake Fairview. Signed, Xavier."

It was very obvious to me at this time, after studying the confession, that this was not a valid case against my court appointed client. It would not take legal wizardry, a UF law degree, or legal experience at that time to free Xavier. It was common sense. I relaxed and reflected on the realities of the evidence which ultimately exonerated Xavier. The so-called "confession" or "admission" written in English legalese by a law enforcement officer were not in the words of a manual laborer who barely spoke English. Xavier was told to sign a piece of paper. He did sign his name but he did not understand what was written on the paper. He could not say those words, much less read them.

I argued to the jury that there was no reason to disbelieve Xavier was walking from work and was merely headed home. It wasn't proven beyond a shadow of a doubt that he committed any crime at all, much less this car burglary. I saw in the jurors' eyes that they understood. I saw the judge nodding slightly. In 20 minutes, the jury came back with those sweet words, "Not guilty." The jurors, the court personnel, and ultimately the judge agreed there was no way that the statement, which previously had seemed so damning, was that of Xavier.

In speaking to the jurors in the hallway afterwards, they were upset that law enforcement seemed to have forced this young man to sign a confession which contained formal language totally foreign to a non-English speaking person. The jurors told me they did not find the seemingly damning signed confession to be authentic after I pointed out the language discrepancy.

This was my first not guilty verdict. It was a big deal. As the attorney,

I was so ecstatic that I won the trial. I also was in awe of the principled young man who rolled the dice with very high stakes. If the jury had come back with a guilty verdict, he would certainly have been sent to prison, and not vindicated. What I remember most is this kid's iron clad principles and his willingness to stick by the truth.

Criminal defense lawyers are a different breed of cat. With all the pop culture about the legal system, lawyers now aren't always looking for justice so much as looking for a good social media post, or a reason to get airtime on a local television station or podcast. Legal proceedings have become a big sport now, with both sides committed to a win-at-all-costs mentality. There's a lot of icing and less cake these days in terms of justice. If we win, we have our chests puffed out. We won because we are amazing and turned the right screws at just the right time. If we lose a trial, it's because the evidence was overwhelming, the jurors made a piss-poor decision, the jury wasn't paying attention, or the jury was lazy and just wanted the decision to be made. It's never our fault if we lose. The loser, of course, is the unfairly accused.

In the case of Xavier, my client was innocent and we proved it. Most of my clients, however, are not innocent of wrongdoing.

The vast majority of my efforts and energy goes towards coming up with an appropriate sentence for the behavior of my clients. There are rote ways that prosecutors and judges utilize to determine sentences. One is a score sheet. In the State of Florida, certain crimes carry certain points. Score sheets assess prior criminal history, the "level" of the charged crime, and such things as whether a victim was injured, whether or not the offender was on probation at the time, and other criterion. An accumulated 44 points gets prison time ... period. Defense attorneys believe it gives judges and prosecutors comfort in having cold calculations, numerical equations, as a guide to how much prison time a person should receive. So, a prosecutor can say, "Well, Mr. Smith scores 88 months to 110 months, so offer him the 88 months." Sounds reasonable and fair, right? Wrong! Every case with every set of circumstances and personal history is unique. Often there is a fine line between a charge that does carry enough points to warrant a prison sentence and a different event or named crime that does not carry a prison sentence. At that point, the war effort for a rabid defense attorney is to convince the judge and prosecutor to label the illicit behavior of the client as having committed the lesser of the offenses, to get a non-incarceration sentence for instance.

A client retired from the court system for example. She had a daughter who was a drug addict. The daughter got popped trafficking heroin which carries a minimum of three years in jail depending on the weight of the drugs, even though it was not her vehicle where the drugs were found. She's not innocent. She admitted the drugs were hers so we were not going to trial. The goal was to get the charge down to possession with intent to distribute, which carries probation, not prison. The same set of circumstances with different legal labeling of the behavior got her a lesser sentence.

I believe most American citizens with any compassion for humanity, would want a woman who had never sold drugs, but had a horrific heroin addiction, to remain in the community. There, she could stay employed and get help, as opposed to being housed in a prison 15 years at a cost to taxpayers by virtue of a number spit out of a calculator.

I gladly represent both innocent people and guilty people. I give each person a personalized solution for their legal entanglement, always looking for the best possible outcome,

CHAPTER 25, TAHITIAN TALE

During my early career, while the sharks continued circling in the Orlando courtrooms, I indulged in two weeks of vacation ... to relax.

I jerked my surfboard towards me and climbed back on it preparing to paddle. My heart was pounding loudly over the smashing waves. Blood was seeping from my feet and legs where they were sliced by the coral reef. I bent my knees and positioned my bloody dripping feet as far over my back as I could. The blood was pooling in the small of my back. I sensed danger nearby. Sharks can smell blood a few hundred meters away which triggers their hunter instincts to seek the wounded for food. I was wounded. The nature I was so enthralled with a few moments prior had now become my mortal enemy. Time was of the essence to get out of the water. My own head was yelling, "Shit! I fucked up again!"

Waterman who revel in adventure, generally travel with surfing, diving or fishing buddies and end up with remarkable tantalizing stories. On this trip, I ended up alone in the water. I went to Tahiti with an attorney who did not surf, dive or fish. He was not interested in watersports. He occupied himself with chasing women while I chased waves.

The journey took 22 hours to fly from Orlando to Los Angeles, then to Tahiti, then on a small plane to the island of Moorea. The puddle jumper airline tried to reject my surfboard on the last flight to Moorea but with a generous cash tip I prevailed and my board made it intact.

In my mind Club Med stood for travel in too organized of a fashion. Club Med had set meal hours, a planned activity schedule, and an orchestrated song and dance routine to begin and end each day. Adhering to time schedules for fun-in-a-can activities was not my style, especially on vacation. My work schedule in the late 1980s was regimented and on this vacation, I craved freedom.

With my first glance around, my premature contempt for the Club Med concept dissipated. Stunning women buzzed around all of the fake fun activity spots. I would later find out they were from Australia, France, England, Brazil, New York, California, and many other places I had never been. The beauties were alluring but the island adventure I found even more intriguing.

The very first day after the mediocre breakfast, I opted out of the nature hike. I went in search of more rigorous action away from the Club Med property. On the van ride into the resort, I noticed some local Tahitians playing soccer on a sports field of grass and dirt. Wanting to get fresh air and get my heart pumping after the excruciating flights, I walked to the nearby field. I accepted their cheerful nonverbal invitation to join in on their game. Soccer has global universal rules. Most every player and most every team has a unique style of play, but those styles of play do not vary radically. What did vary about this game was that nobody spoke English other than a few words. That was of no consequence.

After the friendly match, a kid motioned me to follow him to his thatched roof, open air hut, to have water and a local juice concoction. I wanted to know his opinion of how I fared in the neighborhood soccer match. His response was to point at my mid-section as he dead-panned, "Too much beer." This kid on this faraway dot island discerned I was a boozer just that quickly. I chuckled to myself.

My new friend looked like Mobley in "Jungle Book." His name sounded something like Mobley and it was close enough for us to communicate. Out of the corner of my eye, I saw Mobley had two surfboards in the grass patch behind his hut. I sprinted over to them and held one up. I pointed alternately to the board and Mobley and kept repeating, "You surf? You surf?"

After several minutes navigating our language barrier, I was fairly certain we had arranged to go surfing the next day. The best I could decipher was that he designated 9 a.m. as the meeting time.

So, on day two of the Club Med stay, I took my six- foot-four-inch Florida-shape and made the 300-yard trek again to the village. Mobley was nowhere to be seen. When I started to poke around his neighborhood, the men folk began to mosey out of their huts and eye me suspiciously. I was jonesing for surf so I paced back to the roadside to the entry of the village and just waited ... and waited ... and waited.

An hour later Mobley showed up for our surf session. He looked at my board and smirked and mumbled something in his Polynesian language. He started walking north. Without a word spoken, I just fell in behind him. The occasional car would breeze by us. This local didn't stick out his thumb or forefinger like they do in the U.S. Virgin Islands. He didn't hitchhike. He just walked. I walked, too.

Then a VW van buzzed by us and stopped on the side of the road ahead of us. My local friend slid his board in the van and gave a hearty hello to the driver who was friendly to him but glared at me without a smile. In about half an hour we pulled up to the parking lot of a break which I later learned was called Ha'Piti.

We got ourselves and three boards out of the van. My companions strapped their leashes to their left ankles. This hinted to me that the waves in this area might break from right to left. As I was putting my leash on my right ankle, I was studying the water and what I assumed would be our paddle out to the surf.

It turns out that Ha'Piti is a wave that forms and breaks over a barrier reef. So, we paddled a better part of a mile across a lagoon around coral reefs towards the motherlode. When I got halfway to the actual surf break, a panic started to overtake my reality. I was 3,000 miles from home. I was paddling into big, dangerous surf with people I did not know and didn't even speak the same language. Additionally, I had not bothered to tell anyone where I was going. What in the hell was I thinking?

Any seasoned surfer will tell you there was no way I was going to turn around and flake out on this surf. What was most terror-inducing was not the foreign venue or the unknown below the surface, but what was becoming the known fact. With each stroke closer to the takeoff zone, the waves came into focus and they were getting bigger, and bigger, and bigger. The Tahitians who learned on these waves at their home break were completely unfazed. They were whooping and laughing the entire time.

When we got to the critical point of Ha'Piti, Mobley spun his gun-shaped board into a giant left-hander. The face was 20-feet and he rode it 300-yards before I saw him leap off the back of the wave. There were only six people in the water but I did not dare paddle into any of these wedges for 45 minutes. When I did, it was just a shoulder of the wave maybe ten-feet in the face and I resigned myself to a shorter 150-yard ride.

For a Florida boy this was Nirvana, a Nirvana with an edge. I was getting slung across razor sharp reefs at speeds I had never experienced. With each ride my confidence was growing. The big problem was apparent though. My Florida board, shaped for up to four-foot surf, was woefully ill equipped for these waves. I finally had the guts to take off on a smaller wave from the main peak with the face still 15-feet, and I lost control of my yellow Natural Art halfway through the ride. I took a serious tumble. Mercifully, I was spared the reef.

What did happen was equally as perilous. Shortly after I hit the water, I felt the release of the weight of the leash on my ankle. My leash broke.

Once I got my breath, I scanned around for my board. I couldn't see it. I swam as hard as I could for the channel in which we had paddled out. My new acquaintances were watching my misadventure closely but did not make any moves to help me. After swimming toward the shore along the channel, and scanning the reef for my board, I finally spotted it. It was getting beat to hell on dry coral about 75-yards away from me. Halfway to the board, I let my guard down, and pushed my feet down to see how deep the water was. I was immediately sliced by coral. I was panic stricken again. I got cut badly four more times before I reached the board and climbed on it for the half mile paddle back to the launching place on shore.

Some Tahitian fishermen were watching my risky situation go down and they were more helpful than the surfers. They cranked up their kicker motor, eased towards me and let me climb clumsily into their small fishing boat. The blood splattered against the bottom of the small wood vessel as I fell inside. I was whipped and too exhausted to sit up. They whistled to get my attention and pointed at a massive dorsal fin cruising not far from where I retrieved my board. The danger I had sensed now had a visible triangle shape to confirm my fear.

Sleepy predictable Club Med suddenly seemed adventurous enough to me for the rest of the two weeks. I had a fresh surf story to add to my life story, and most importantly to entertain the gorgeous women at the all-inclusive resort.

I was glad to be alive. I heard the Moorea Club Med did not fare as well over time. It closed after tourism declined after 9/11. The one in Bora Bora closed, too. Things do not last forever. I am happy I took time to travel when opportunity presented itself. But the one thing that was emphatically affirmed to me on that trip about adventure travel is ... solo surfing sucks.

My friend asked if I would do it again. My life patterns speak for themselves. Yes, I would paddle back out even in Tahiti. Life is full of surprises. Some surprises suck like when Ma Ocean presents rogue sets or surprise finned visitors. Then again, some surprises suck even more than others. I would soon have a surprise I could have never imagined knocking at my front door.

CHAPTER 26, BUSTED

I was 30, loving life and always up for travel and adventure. In the late 1990s, I closed shop for mini lobster season which is the last consecutive Wednesday and Thursday of July each year. A group of my law school buddies invited me to Palm Beach. These South Florida guys liked to use scuba gear and explore the bottom for lobster antenna coming out of the bottom of the reefs to bag their limits. I wasn't so comfortable with the scuba idea. I had done it but wasn't certified and not familiar enough with the equipment to be safe. Nonetheless, not wanting to be deemed a pansy, I geared up clumsily, walked to the edge of a 28-foot Contender anchored within view of the shoreline and plunked into the water backwards. I did so only because I saw Jacques Cousteau on TV dive in that way. I began the hunt. Unfortunately, the wind and current churned up the water so visibility was nil. In fact, as I was swimming through the water with borrowed fins, I lost my sense of direction. Looking for clear water, I swam face first into the sandy bottom forcing my mask to bang against my face and popping the regulator out of my mouth. I was glad nobody saw my snafu. That was enough for me. I followed the bubbles to the top and awkwardly climbed into the boat. It was tough-sledding for the first day of lobster season. I caught zero lobster. So, we went to catch a buzz. We partied a few days away including a trip to the Cheetah strip club.

I had to get back for work. I was hungover and high driving back over two hours to my friendly confines. I finally made it to my tenth-floor condo all sunburned and hot. I was living at Downtown Towers in Orlando. At that time there were only a few high-rise condos before it was hip and cool to live in soaring luxury buildings. I had a sweeping view for miles of the flat terrain over the tops of the oaks. Even with that epic view, I did not see what was coming my way.

At 3 a.m., the condo concierge downstairs called my unit on a land line and said that someone had backed into my car and I needed to come down immediately. I felt like dog shit from all the partying. I pushed back and said that I would handle it later, but he insisted. I reluctantly threw on some sandy clothes with my hair sticking out all over. I was half asleep.

When I opened my door, a dozen plain-clothed cops had their guns drawn. They were pointing the guns directly at me. I was high, so the light bulb didn't go off right away. I was busted. I thought I was being abducted so I resisted at first. It was a feeble attempt at resistance. They had me on the ground with arms behind my back secured in handcuffs in short order. As the men came into focus, I recognized one was from the Seminole County Sheriff's Office. Even though I was living in Orange County, the alleged illegal activity was going on in Seminole County. The CCIB or City County Investigative Bureau headed up the investigation out of Seminole County. Since it was a federal issue, numerous groups had their hands in it. Guns were raised by the FBI, MBI or Metropolitan Bureau of Investigation, Orange County Sherriff's Office, and Seminole County Sherriff's Office.

The Seminole County Sherriff liked me for some reason. I saw him around the courts. He didn't let his boys tear up the condo or punch holes in the wall like a normal search. They had a search warrant for the condo. They found what they were looking for. They made a beeline for my master closet like they had been in my place before and found cocaine immediately as if they knew where it was. At first, I thought someone had told them. Now I know most people keep cash or dope in the pockets of suitcoat jackets. I was not unique in my tactic to hide my stash. The Sheriff took me into custody and personally drove me to the jail.

My life flashed before my eyes like I was about to die. I did feel like I was dying inside. Like thousands of arrested citizens before me, I was holding out the slimmest of hopes that this was a horrible yet realistic nightmare, but it was real. It was real and really terrifying. With all the prior illegal activities, this was the first time I was actually caught and arrested.

All I could think about was my parents. They had already endured the ramifications of so much of my errant and risky behavior and my generally known reputation for overdoing everything mind-altering. The news of this arrest, and it would be in the news in all forms, would be utterly devastating to my parents. I was in excruciating emotional pain thinking of how much heartache and anguish I caused these good people. I cannot rightfully deny that I did not age them and take years off their dear lives. My embarrassment would be known to the whole town. The local newspaper did an outstanding job of covering every gritty detail of my arrest and dug up details of my personal history. The television stations equally reported on the details of my incarceration. It was a life changing moment and the moment was memorialized in news media.

Law enforcement thought they were going to hit a home run when they obtained a warrant to search my residence. The Feds had a wiretap on a guy and suspected they would eventually hear my voice. I met the Italian in Orlando through a girl I dated long distance when I was in law school. I slowly warmed up to him and we became good friends. He was a Mafia-type. He was a good connection for coke and I trusted him. When law enforcement heard me utter the number 14 on a recorded phone conversation to this guy, they wrongly assumed it was 14 kilos of coke. In fact, I had been moving more than that at any given time with Luke out of U.S.V.I. but they were about two years too late. What they found was a bag of mere grams. The irony was overwhelming that I had run serious quantities of coke dealing drugs and now got popped with a small amount I was using recreationally. The actual dope running was in the rearview mirror. I was just a guy with a drug habit with a personal stash and some bad luck.

Law enforcement also was giddy about busting a criminal defense attorney. Well, they got Jack on that detail. I went through the jail process and went to court in handcuffs the next day. When I was ushered into the courtroom in Federal Court in shackles and prison blues, I was in pure shock. The sitting judge readily released me from incarceration with just my signature. I did not post bail. They knew I wasn't going anywhere.

I hired a lawyer friend about my age cutting his teeth in federal court. I didn't shop around for legal representation. I didn't think I was going to prison. Other guys at the time got community control or house arrest and probation with the same weight as I had. Federal court however has a much higher conviction rate with better trained, more sophisticated investigators to make cases stick. They have the resources of the U.S. government behind them. In federal court the chips are stacked against the accused. It didn't help that the Italian got popped with a ton of product and the only way out for him was to rat people out to the Feds. I was miserable waiting for the chips to fall. I'd call the Italian and teasing him would whistle like a songbird. I actually understand why he had to sing. He did what he had to do for himself. He did more time for what Feds defined as a drug conspiracy. The alleged co-conspirators also spilled what they knew about me in order for them to get lesser sentences. It worked.

By the time the law came knocking, I was a drug user, nothing more. My lawyer ran with the idea that I had a substance abuse issue. I could not deny my culpability; I was going to have to pay. The judge could not let me get off easy because the case got too much press and was too high profile.

I was finished with my past but my past wasn't finished with me. All of us had a past. None of us were perfect. Our imperfect pasts knocked on our doors.

CHAPTER 27, BUSTED NOT BROKEN

While waiting for my case to snake its way through the federal system, I didn't know what to do or how to conduct myself for what would be seven months of limbo. Once I got home after the arrest to contemplate my plight, I did the only thing I knew to do. I was innocent until proven guilty. I still had a giant caseload and was still authorized to practice law. So, I marched right in the courthouses and courtrooms to represent people accused of crimes in the State of Florida until the day I was sentenced to prison time. On the day I relinquished my right to practice law in the State of Florida for three long years, people around me, other attorneys and judges were both shocked and impressed that I kept my business going. Surreal is not the right word. I don't know if there is an accurate word to describe my lot in life between the Downtown Tower raid and the sentencing date. Other lawyers who were honest commented that I had a large set of balls to show up again. I had a booming practice. I was going to keep it going until I was a convicted felon and it was mandatory for me to terminate my practice. There was always a chance that would not happen.

Not only was I in denial, but so were new clients. I gave current and new clients the option to stay with the firm despite my personal problems and let my partner handle their cases in the event that I could not. Only three clients abandoned ship. The whole ordeal was mind-blowing.

Other lawyers were aghast that I had been arrested. Other lawyers were aghast that I was still practicing law. Other lawyers were very, very aghast that new clients were pouring in the door. Yes, I was open for business. I had the option to mope or to go out with a bang and not a whimper. I chose a big bang and the cases just kept coming.

My negative publicity and turmoil turned into Jay's good fortune. Jay was my business partner at the time and an outstanding litigator, but he, too, was thirsty. Not surprisingly, being in my inner circle, he was an alcoholic and partier. He was drinking by mid-morning each day. Lawyers can be notorious drunks and in criminal defense work, it's rampant. He just could not handle the volume of business for the long run. For the time I would later be in prison, it was gratifying to me for him to be a pen pal of sorts while he minded the store.

It was shortly after this time period that Jay had a jet ski accident on a nearby lake and he suffered severe brain damage. At the time of his accident, he had 0.36 blood alcohol level. Some humans could die just having that much booze in their system. Jay never was the same. Unfortunately, Jay died of an alcohol overdose ten years later.

Between the arrest and looming prison time, I practiced law with reckless abandon. I was unnaturally aggressive. That's not really my normal style, but I was angry at myself and angry at the world. I went to trial on any case I thought I could possibly win or I could get dismissed on a technicality. My theory was that I had nothing to lose. You know what? It worked.

I got caught up in the practice of law and concentrated on my cases. I would get in a good mood and start laughing and being at ease, then reality would shake me about my pending fate.

While I did march back into the courtroom with my federal case pending, I did not want to socialize at first with the legal community. People love to watch others fall from grace. Out of sheer embarrassment I kept a low public profile when I realized my mess was not a fictional nightmare but a shit-storm reality. When I got arrested, the story was all over the local rags and television news. My predicament was no secret. I became famous, or infamous in my case, with one big news headline.

My friends encouraged me to get out and I reluctantly agreed. To my complete surprise, people did not run away but instead leaned-in for bits and pieces. I became a local minor celebrity in the limelight in a horrible way. I anticipated that I was a leper for life but my predicament had the opposite effect. Some girls walked up and kissed me even. Lots of people asked lots of prying intrusive questions. People wanted to know who snitched. They wanted gory details. People were bloodthirsty for gossip. Even the Winter Park bubble people who only appear to socialize in their own zip code engaged me. I imagine fresh gossip in that small stuck-up village is a hot commodity. Whether they were supportive or not, I was sought out for entertainment. I got bored with repeating the story so many times, so I embellished at times, adding that I fought the cops at the raid which I did not. People were salivating for tidbits of my ordeal. I dished out the dirt and they ate it up heartily. The attention and openly talking about the situation somehow relieved some of the pain. My star faded and the bust was old news by the time I got out of prison.

CHAPTER 28, WAIT, GAVEL, WAIT, TRAVEL

A lot of pain was heading my way in two distinct major waiting periods.

It was not a foregone conclusion that I would go to prison. In the back of my mind I held out a realistic hope that I would not be locked up at all. What makes being in this situation agonizing is that you do not know. In the state courts, you can more easily anticipate what to expect for an outcome. In federal courts, it is different. The judges like to decide. It was severely emotionally painful waiting for the gavel to bang.

Months after the arrest, the judge ended the mystery on the morning of my sentencing. The hope that I would remain in my community at home on house arrest and / or probation to serve my sentence was stomped out with the judge's order. Boom. Prison. I was sent up the river. He declared I would spend 15 months in the bureau prisons. The air went out of the defense side of the courtroom who had lobbied for house arrest. The prosecutor side could barely contain their excitement for the pending lock up of a lawyer. A few months of my life in federal prison ... there it was ... the answer I didn't want but at least the waiting was over.

The second waiting period was for another few months before I turned myself in to prison. The judge ordered that I could self-report for my term of incarceration. It was up to the bureau of prisons to decide which location where I was to be housed. I was further tortured inside waiting for them to determine where I was to go. It was ultimately decided I would travel to an Air Force Base in the Florida Panhandle.

During my time preparing and my time away, my friends told people I was in England. I am lucky to have a circle of loyal friends. Getting ready to accept my fate was a maddening and frightening experience. I was warned I would get butt raped, ass kicked, and the guards would treat me like dirt. Others said I could get easy access to drugs, conjugal visits and rounds of golf. Neither of the extremes were true. When the waiting was going down, it was hard for me to have optimistic thoughts.

If I knew 30 years later, that I could look back and that was a small part of my life, I would have felt better. If I knew that back then that a good life would follow, I wouldn't have worried as much. But then, oh yes, then I was worried.

CHAPTER 29, PRISON

Jack Wander was stripped of his name, his lawyer title, and most of his dignity. Jack was now awarded a Federal Prison identification ten-digit number. February of the year after my sentencing, I turned myself in to the designated prison at an Air Force Base. There are several federal prisons on military bases and the Federal Bureau of Prisons assigned me to this one. I called the place England, in sync with the cover story that my friends created for my time away from home.

It turns out, I got a soft prison experience with a white painted line as a barrier, but no bars. I was a first-time non-violent offender and my psychological and social background check showed that I was not a threat to flee or to do violence to anyone.

The logistics of my 15-month sentence was unique in that I turned myself in and took myself to prison. More typically in state court, a defendant sentenced to prison time is taken into custody from the courtroom and they are transported while uncomfortably handcuffed in a Department of Corrections van. The van, referred to as diesel therapy by lawyers, makes stops for prisoners to stay overnight in various county jails until the final destination.

I had the advantage mentally and emotionally of thoroughly eyeballing England. I drove to the Florida Panhandle the day before I was to turn myself in to look at where I was to be incarcerated. What stood out to me was there were tan physically fit men walking around, working out in an up-to-date weight shack, and playing tennis on four tennis courts. The men seemed cordial towards one another. I was encouraged and relieved by what I saw.

That night I went out in the local town and got trashed. I dined on the finest seafood I could find. I had no idea what quality of food or, for that matter, what quality of life I would have for the upcoming months.

The next day I turned myself in, and like all other important days of my life, I was very hungover. I had been careful not to do any coke or other drugs pending my surrender because I knew I would be tested. Hungover and slightly buzzed, the turning in process was horrifying. There was a female guard who took and searched the belongings I was permitted to bring to the facility. I had with me two pairs of tennis shoes, one watch, eyeglasses, one suit of clothing for visitation days, and a tennis racquet.

This was all tucked in my trusty turquoise Adidas athletic bag which previously was used to transport dope.

Prior to incarceration I had been bombarded and mentally tortured by stories of this initial reception at the prison. The female guard was pleasant as we filled out numerous forms by hand going over personal and medical history. As she finished paperwork and cursory search of my belongings, the corrections officer looked uncomfortable and started to look around the area seemingly for assistance. It was time for my full body cavity search. In the very short time she had to acquaint herself with me, I had impressed her enough that she sought out a male prison guard to do the honors. It may have been something the gal said to the male officer or that he could tell I was not going to be a rule-breaker or trouble maker. The anal portion of the full body check search was also cursory... thankfully.

From there I was led to my dorm. Now my head was really spinning out of control. I was in prison. The guard led me to quarters which housed 40 men in one large room with bunk style beds. As I checked in it was midday and the majority of the inmates were at their jobs so the dorm was empty. The dorm was incredibly immaculate. Every bed was made military style. I could see my reflection in the well-polished floors. There was no stench in the air as I had imagined it would be. There was not a bleach smell either, just the vaguest hint of soaps and deodorants wafting from the bathrooms. Each cubby area had two twin bunk beds. Two inmates shared a desk. The guard pointed me to my cubby and top bunk. My eyes were drawn to the desk to be shared with my bunkmate. To my greatest surprise and relief there were two magazines, National Geographic and SURFER. I could not believe my eyes. The sight was so welcoming in the most unwelcoming of situations. What I presumed was that my bunkmate was an intellectual surfer. I could have done backflips back to Orlando. A normal state prison is an animalistic, dirty nightmare. This federal prison, by contrast, was neat and clean. I began to hope the other inhabitants were halfway normal.

After I placed my belongings where the corrections officer showed me, he asked if I had eaten lunch. He ordered me to go to chow hall and then to report back for orientation within two hours.

I said, "Yes sir. Where is the chow hall?"

A bit disgustedly he pointed in a general direction and said, "On the other side of the compound."

I thought it was odd that I would just walk by myself. I followed orders and walked in the general direction he had commanded. I exited the dorm door onto an outdoor courtyard that resembled a high school campus. There were a few inmates pruning and clipping the already manicured landscape. The chow hall was a 70-yard walk seemingly through a park from which you could view a weight shack and a large body of water. Chow hall was also empty. I stood dumbfoundedly in front of a cafeteria-style serving section. A cook, also an inmate, spotted me and walked up and cheerfully greeted me with a smile and said, "What are you having today?"

I realized I was going to be alright. A feeling of relief washed over me.

I mumbled an apology. I was so new there and didn't know protocol. I never realized I would have options so I asked, "What are my options?"

He replied, "We still have meatloaf, fried chicken or lasagna. The chicken is popular but I do think the white meat is gone. I made the meatloaf and it's really, really good. We have green beans, mashed potatoes and the salad bar is behind you."

"No shit! He's telling the truth," I thought as I wheeled around to view a full salad bar like the one at Steak and Ale.

The chef's meatloaf was surprisingly gourmet compared to what I had imagined prison food to be. I forced down half of what I had put on my plate. I was so nervous I was unable to eat much.

I beelined back to the bunk area so as not to miss the orientation meeting. By this time, I was over an hour early. I unpacked my few permitted items and just waited until meeting time.

I was led with other new inmates to a meeting room where the rules were explained. I sat next to a disgraced politician from Louisiana, a physician accused of insurance fraud from Virginia, and a handful of dopers from Florida and Georgia. They told us we would be assigned jobs in the next few days. Meanwhile we were tasked with learning the rules of our new dwelling space including protocols for laundry, writing and receiving correspondence, receiving visitors, telephone use, hours of operation for the tennis courts and other recreational facilities, and other rules and expectations of inmates.

After the meeting, I met my bunkmate. It turned out he didn't ever actually surf. He was a pleasant-enough white dude with a strong New

Orleans Cajun accent. I would find out he had a reputation for being a thief even while incarcerated. Since he was friendly enough and helpful enough, I overlooked his imperfection. What would he take from me in prison anyway? He had an aspiration to be a personal trainer upon his release. He taught me how to lift weights. I memorized the regimen and still use to this day. I went to prison bloated from a booze and grease diet at 180 pounds. I came out at 148 pounds with very little body fat.

I have always had a very wide lucky streak and that continued during the prison sentence. There is nobody more poised to have an easy time in a lock-up than an attorney, and a criminal defense attorney at that. Within a week, I had dozens of people talking to me about their various situations. There were inmates with wives divorcing them, or their kids were getting in trouble. With an eye to getting early releases, I found myself drafting post-conviction motions. The inmates needed all manner of counsel and consultation.

As Abraham Lincoln said, "A lawyer's time and advice are his stock in trade."

Hence, I was not about to give away my stock for free. I was never short of commissary items including headphones, unlimited coffee, telephone time and extra uniforms. Ice cream was a common currency. Straight up cash worked, too.

I sharpened my tennis game. We had use of the courts at night and I found a few inmates who could play.

Another one of my passions served me well, my strong soccer background. In addition to a prison camp softball team, we had a prison camp soccer team. I watched them practice for a few days before I decided to join. I hadn't played competitively for several years since college. I underestimated myself. I'm never mentally of the mind that I can kick ass. I'm of the opposite mentality and I question myself. It's a common theme in my life.

I was issued my cleats and this gringo joined the group practice. Just like in golf, or surfing or snow skiing, you can tell a person's skill level in the first few seconds. I could kick with my left and right feet equally when warming up. They also noticed I'd tap the ball and make short passes with the inside of my foot on the arch in a snapping motion. They also noticed when I wanted to put more speed or distance on the ball, I'd use the top of my foot. They had their share of gringos and wannabees try to get in their football circle without much success. So even though I underestimated myself, after the first scrimmage they did not underestimate me at all. They asked me to join their team.

They claimed I had a European style of playing. Latin style is more free-flowing with focus on attack. A European technique has aggressive defense while containing freedom of movement. Most of the soccer players were Cuban or Columbian so they played more in the Latin style. If immigrants get popped in Miami or elsewhere in The States then it's a U.S. offense, so they do time in the U.S. before getting deported. There are many immigrants both legal and illegal in our prison system. When they get out of prison and get deported, they sometimes find a way back. Some of the soccer players had been deported and got back in the U.S. several times.

Not just immigrants, but the U.S. incarcerates a higher percentage of population than any other country in the world. This country is not quite 250 years old. It's an infant. As a country, it's immature. It's a melting pot of a convergence of cultures and a government that tries to regulate everything. I read recently that in 1972 there were 300,000 prisoners and by 2014 there were 2,300,000. Between Jacksonville, Gainesville, and Tallahassee in North Florida it's called the iron triangle. Prisoning people is big business. We have a government that wants to over-regulate which creates the perfect storm to send people to jail. I was now one of the gloomy statistics. Jack Wander, inmate number blah, blah, blah.

Men sent to prison are assigned jobs according to their capabilities. If they have a background in construction, they go to prison and do construction. If they have a background in the food and beverage industry, they cook for inmates. The best cooks achieve the coveted position of cooking for the officers' club. They had no particular placement for suspended lawyers. My intuition to come into the facility drug free, polite and respectful was smart. I was assigned the task of maintaining and landscaping the home of the base commander. The base commander resided in a practical yet aesthetic house sitting directly on a bay on the Florida Panhandle. The grass was perfectly mowed and fertilized to a deep emerald green. The lawn spanned 70 yards from the back of the family home to the bay. The shrubbery was crisply maintained. The plants were not delicate or exotic. They were sturdy and accented perfectly with the vista. My predecessor had done such a stellar job that I inherited a meticulously groomed yard to maintain as my job. I later found out that I was assigned the job because of complete lack of criminal history, educational level, positive results of my psycho-social evaluation, my appearance and how the administrators at the prison evaluated my behavior. I would be working in close proximity to the base commander and his family so they chose this position with great care.

Each morning my civilian supervisor Bob would pick up a group of us in a military transport vehicle, leave the prison grounds and take us into the community two-miles from the prison camp. We had a meeting area of sorts where there were bathrooms, equipment storage facilities to hold mowers and weed eaters and other lawn care necessities. From there we would walk to our assignments. I couldn't believe the level of freedom we were given. I would walk from the meeting spot several hundred yards through neighborhoods where kids were being picked up to go to school, folks were grabbing their morning newspapers and going about their normal lives. The military families went nonchalantly about their business while myself and other inmates were strolling right past them to work in their yards.

To keep the designated yards pristinely mowed, edged and manicured to specifications, realistically it would take about two hours a day. So, we had to think of creative ways to fill our time to make it look like we were always working. It didn't take long to get down the timing of Bob's comings and goings in his government issued truck. When I sensed he was about to arrive, I would start raking up a storm and as soon as I would see the top of the antenna of his truck depart the neighborhood street, I'd go back to the real job of fooling around. All of this was at a grand rate of 35 cents-per-hour which I could save and use upon my departure or use at the prison commissary. At the time, minimum wage was $4.25 per-hour. In the law biz, John Wander charged flat fees that averaged several hundred per hour. By sharp contrast, in prison, I was worth a few cents.

The Gulf War's Desert Storm, in response to Iraq's invasion of Kuwait, was in full force when I was there. Although short in duration and small in scale in terms of war, it resulted in most of the men-folk being off the base in various places of the world carrying out their duties. That left these neighborhoods covered up with young military wives. I was never in the military but I can tell you that these women had a big party attitude. The ladies who were left at home when the men went off to war seemed to love to drink. You would see them often in daylight hours way before 5 o'clock cocktail hour carrying cocktails around from house to house. We prisoners discerned that none of these ladies worked. We figured it must be the military culture.

Next to the base commander's house was a row of smaller houses also on the bay occupied by military personnel of lower rank. Right next to the base commander's house lived Margaret. Her husband was a pilot. Being shy and trying to be the rule follower, I was keeping my eyes to myself. I couldn't help but to glance ever so quickly when Margaret, upon my arrival at the yard, walked to the edge of the bay and have coffee every morning. She wore cut off jean shorts with fringe and tank tops. She walked slowly to the water and slowly back to her house. For the first several weeks I dared not acknowledge her.

First of all, I couldn't believe they let a convicted felon wander loose in their neighborhoods. Secondly, as the base commander's wife and two sons got familiar with me, the sons would engage me with whiffle ball games, ball tossing and soccer practices. The social dynamic was uncomfortable beyond description. The base commander and his wife were friendly enough, but they always made certain by facial expression or vague comments that I should know my place. Per usual, I would drop the lawyer card as often as possible to let them know I was truly harmless. That didn't warm them up to me. My feeling was they had seen so many inmates come and go they didn't bother to get to know us. Like a taxi driver or tour guide, I was expected to be of service and then forgotten and never to be seen again.

Meanwhile, Miss Margaret next door started to wave at me ever so suggestively after the first few weeks. After a month or so she would come out on afternoons about the same time after lunch when we workers would go back to the yards to work. She would appear and do yard work of her own. Apparently, her husband was not of the rank to have a prison-assigned yard man. After enough waves and short smiles back and forth, Margaret strolled over and introduced herself in a southern accent. It scared the daylights out of me. I didn't remember any rules about women. I didn't know how to respond as an inmate. Nonetheless, I gladly introduced myself and went to turn around to go back to my yard duties. She just stood there holding a rake and asked me where I was from. Having achieved several steps and 12 yards of separation from Margaret, I felt more at ease that if anyone was watching, I was well on my property and politely answering questions. She was so pretty. Maybe there were a lot of simple and pretty girls in the world but I hadn't noticed because I was always around the party girls saturated with alcohol. She was so nice. It sounds trite but she was southern nice, it's a special kind of nice. She was thirsty for conversation so we got to know each other quickly. Per usual, it didn't take me long to let her know that in my former life I was a lawyer with a surfing habit. She giggled which made me anxious. She was flirting. It was not my imagination.

"I thought you looked like a surfer boy," she charmed.

I made some small regrettable comment about the beach town where she told me she and her family would vacation in L.A., or Lower Alabama. The term Redneck Riviera is a big joke about the Panhandle beaches.

My heart was racing for many reasons. While she was alluring, I couldn't get away quickly enough. Most men analyze encounters with women when they are over, wondering how they fared to the fairer sex. Something about this blunt meeting and my rapid departure made me feel buoyant. I had female conversation other than with guards. It was not smart behavior. Pushing the limits could get me in worse trouble than I already was.

One really good thing about having civilian supervisors on these off-prison-site assignments, is that they could be easily bribed. These guys, mostly country boys, were making minimum wage. So, if an inmate wanted to he could get booze, pot, other contraband or even sexual encounters. It could be arranged through Bob. I would ultimately bribe Bob for him to merely absent himself and look away at certain prearranged times.

I rapidly felt I was running the show at the prison. In two short months, I'd gotten to know everything about the place. I was now captain of the soccer team and practically practicing law for other inmates at a high rate of pay according to prison standards. Right about the same time, on the job at the house, I was walking the perimeter of the yard fertilizing and heard a hissing sound. It was Miss Margaret holding out a Budweiser can with drops of condensation falling off of it just like it came out of an ice-cold cooler. Frozen, I quickly calculated when Bob would be coming around again. I did a wide scan of the base commander's yard to see if the occupants were home. I acted boldly. I took about 20 quick steps directly towards the Alabama girl and reached for the beer in her hand. Right as my hand touched the cold beer, her other arm wrapped around my waist and she pulled me to hide in the side door of her garage. She kissed me. We kissed for about a minute. I didn't realize how starved I was for human contact. It wasn't just a kiss. It was a reminder of something I was missing. The beer was still intact and unopened. For once in my life, something superseded the craving for a sip of beer. I smiled and ran back to my equipment. For the rest of that shift, every time I walked past that door, we looked at each other and laughed hysterically. I don't know what was so funny but we had the same reaction.

When I was up close I could see she had brown eyes. They twinkled. She was even sweeter somehow up close. She had soft skin like a child. She was only 21-years-old. She had come from one of those little towns in the South with a military base close by where the grand prize was to marry a military man. She hit the jackpot with a pilot. She married him within four months of meeting him, without really knowing him. She was miserable in her marriage. She was smart but grew up with no money and no opportunity to make something of herself. She was so lost and so young. I was no better. I was lost. Being lost together somehow made my time in England more bearable. The affair I had with her was probably not her first or her last. There were several of these types of encounters with other local women by other inmates. It was common at that prison.

There were two other Orlando drug dopers that passed through there during my time. I wasn't happy they got busted, I would never wish that on anyone, but I have to admit it was comforting to see familiar faces in such a surreal setting.

I met a plethora of mobsters and derelicts during my prison time. When I finished my time and later got my law license back, the inmates rang my phone off the hook each time they needed legal advice for themselves and their friends. There were a number of frequent flyers that I represented several times.

I was devastated that I had my freedom taken away at the prison. I do believe, however, that it made me a better lawyer in the long run. I have empathy for the anxieties, fears, and concerns of my clients that I just could not get any other way.

CHAPTER 30, LIMBO TO LITIGATION

I was released from prison after serving my term. I had culture shock. I was no longer confined. I had freedom, but not quite complete freedom yet. I was in limbo passing my time in a mundane, vanilla very supervised way.

It was mandatory as part of my probation for me to have full time employment so I sold time shares. I also did landscaping, delivered beverages, and accepted almost any employment to satisfy my probation officer.

After my prison sentence, I successfully completed supervised release or probation in a year and a half. There is no rhyme or reason for the timing, but my three-year probation was thankfully cut in half.

After that, I convinced the Governor of Florida to reinstate my civil rights through a petition for clemency. Once I had my civil rights restored, which are the right to vote, hold political office, and all civil rights we Americans hold dear, I now had the prerequisite to ask for my law license. I went through the arduous process to petition reinstatement to The Florida Bar.

One fateful day, I was in the bank parking lot going to deposit some meager checks. My cell phone rang. The call was from the office of the Tallahassee lawyer who specialized in Florida Bar discipline cases. I hired him to get me through the process of becoming a lawyer again. He was a great guy and even had visited me at England. The voice on the other end was the lawyer's secretary advising me that my license to practice law had been reinstated. I was readmitted to The Florida Bar.

The impact of that day was momentous. The astonishing news out of the blue brought me to my knees and to tears. In one unexpected instant with that electrifying phone call, I was a lawyer standing in that parking lot with all the rights and privileges "thereunto appertaining." The Supreme Court of Florida runs on its own schedule and it made the decision to let me practice law without warning. I went from zero to 120 mph in the blink of an eye. I was a lawyer again. It was scintillating. I was fully engaged. I was a good lawyer with a screwed up personal life. I was coming out of a several-year struggle in an instant. I was hungry and anxious to engage in high impact litigation. I was also extremely insecure.

Thoughts of uncertainty whirled through my brain, "Would anyone hire me? Would I be able to perform as before? How would the judges receive me? Would prosecutors treat my clients unfairly because of my own dramatic controversial history? Where to begin? What now?"

As far as I knew, no law firms were hiring convicted felons and there was no how-to book on reopening a law practice after closing for several years. I sped to the Orange County Bar Association office on Orange Avenue and picked up the monthly periodical. This is before the internet, so I relied on the newsletter for job opening notices.

One ad screamed out at me as a way to ease back into the legal profession. It read, "Lawyer needed to cover traffic infraction hearings paid by the case." I responded immediately and set up an interview with a kindly gentleman. He set up some basic framework for people to hire him, to defend them against speeding charges and the like. He had a smooth system in place to get clients through the legal system. He needed a lawyer to go to the judges to resolve simple traffic infraction matters. The pay rate was $50 per-hearing. Solid Gold! He hired me on the spot and gave me a handful of files to march into court the next day. He had studied me in what would loosely be called a job interview. He didn't ask many questions, just went into the tasks at hand. After he handed me the files, he remarked, "I hear you are a solid lawyer." I thought my heart, my brain and my balls would all explode at the same time. I needed an affirmation desperately to offset the insecurity that had built up in my absence from the law.

I practically fell down the steps of his rag-tag office in downtown Orlando with the files, got into my Z car, and raced home to resurrect a decent suit for court appearances. The reception of me at the courthouse, at downtown corner cafes, and every little locale around downtown Orlando was remarkably positive and loving. People forgive. People forget. My confidence built back with each of the offerings of kind words.

Before long, the juicy new criminal cases started flying at me. In response, I quickly opened my own office once again near the Orlando courthouse. In addition to accepting criminal cases, out of fear and economic insecurity, I also practiced threshold law which is a legal cliché for taking any case that walks in the door.

One of the areas I became proficient at was divorce law. I became proficient at litigating divorce cases, but I hated them. As a sole practitioner, the ability to litigate a family law case is a handy arrow to have in your quiver. Representing both citizens accused of crimes and folks wanting a divorce seemed to flow together well for me. I represented a few high-profile contentious divorces with intense litigation.

Ironically, the Assistant U.S. Attorney who brought the indictment against me and prosecuted me criminally on my cocaine charges which sent me to prison, came to me to represent him in his contentious divorce case. After we had opposed each other on opposite sides of the legal universe, years later we were both in private practice and had entirely different roles with each other in the legal system.

Courthouses have rumor mills. Courthouses are rumor mills. Mystically results of cases filter through the legal community. Somehow, the outcome of cases, especially with intense litigation, also filter into the community at large. Since my client was a well-known lawyer and he had won his case, if there is a win with a divorce, the news of my adept lawyering in divorce court spread quickly. Those cases solidified my second avenue of law to keep my business flowing. If I became nervous about my finances at any time, I could take on another hated divorce war. Jack Wander was just good at it. Being a good manipulator, I knew which screws to turn to get the judge's attention. It worked. So, I had the luxury of limiting my new threshold practices to criminal cases and divorce cases. My calendar was full.

CHAPTER 31, GETTING HIGH AND GETTING BY

Within two years of rehanging my law license in my Orlando office, business was exploding. I had a heavy docket today. I was due in front of five different judges in two different counties. Every event was scheduled for 9 a.m. Typically I would have other lawyers stand in for me or would have called the judges in advance to tell them I may be late and had to stagger my schedule. I had done neither in preparation for this day. I had done neither because the tequila beckoned intensely for the previous four days. Thankfully in more lucid days prior I had prepared for these clients causes by way of research and negotiations with familiar prosecutors.

I picked out a suit, a sturdy Hart Shaffner and Marx in a tropical weight wool, that had brought great luck previously in the courtroom. When I looked in the mirror, I desperately needed a shave and a miracle cure for the dark, dark circles under my eyes. I started the shower to begin the beautification process. I shave in the shower. Big problem, I was shaking so badly from alcohol withdrawal that I could not properly put a razor accurately to my face. I turned off the steamy shower and found a near empty vodka bottle in my kitchen and turned it up and took three hard gulps. Within ten minutes, I was shaving somewhat with precision. The shakes were diminished and the blood of life was starting to pump back into my swollen face. It is that way with active hard-core alcoholics. The counter intuitive morning drink will give the energy, confidence and fortitude to get into the day. It's a blood alcohol level science phenomenon.

I opted to show up in the courtroom of the meanest and strictest judge first. Pedro was to enter a plea to Grand Theft Auto, receive probation, and pay for the damage he had done to a stolen vehicle. This was simple enough, standard stuff in my world, but I now had the frightening prospect confronting me to address the podium and talk to the judge. To enter the plea, I was required to fill out by hand a written plea form. The form advised the court that the client knew he was foregoing a trial and taking the deal. The terrifying problem that now confronted me was that the medicinal effect of those giant slugs of vodka was wearing off quickly. I could not write. My hands were trembling so anything I attempted to put to paper was completely illegible scrawl. This basic routine task was now insurmountable.

Per usual, being a manipulator, I figured out a solution using my friend circle. I scanned the courtroom and saw a friendly face in the crowd of my long-time friend Lance. His nickname was Lance Studrock. This guy had it all. He was studly, smart and successful. He was always dressed to the nines like right out of GQ Magazine. He was a good human being. He was a partier, too, so I knew he would be sympathetic to my cause. I nodded and motioned for him to go outside with plea form in hand ready to be filled out. I lied my ass off to Lance. I told him I had sprained my wrist playing softball the night before and could not write and asked if he would fill out the form. Lance being my friend, obliged readily with growing concern behind his glasses as he handed the form back to me. I suspected he knew I was lying. I also assumed the fumes emanating from me were making their way to his nostrils. He seemed so clean, clear and happy to me. I envied the fact that he could write crisply on this day. He wrote everything down as I dictated. Pedro and I did our thing with the stickler we called Judge Hatchett. Then I left for my next scary assignment. All assignments on this day were terrifying due to alcohol toxicity.

A sadder day to me was ahead. Within ten days of Lance helping me navigate Judge Hatchett, he would die. He was addicted to cocaine. He was in the office by himself, I'm not sure exactly what happened, but he hit his head on the corner of the desk. The guy who was a friend to everyone died at a young age all by himself.

Another attorney friend died around that same time of a heart attack while he was detoxing. I tried to help Mack through several detoxes. The last time, he was so jaundiced from his liver failing that his eyes looked like lemon wedges. He was a great guy, too. The field of law created or brought out alcoholism. It was rampant.

Many of my friends from high school, college, law school and early career, declined over the years, turned cray-cray, did off-the-chain partying with DUI after DUI, or actually died. Many of my friends were drinking, snorting and smoking. Some drank themselves onto the streets. It is impossible to describe. In the face of certain disaster, we would not stop. The consequences just did not matter when getting high was the sole focus. I'm living proof.

Alcoholics tend to be talented. I grew up thinking an alcoholic was someone who had a paper bag around a beer and lived under a bridge. Alcoholics generally are talented in some area. It's perplexing. We can be successful to the outside world, and we can conceal a shitload of bad behavior. For example, I left the Brevard County Justice Center recently after a morning hearing. The courthouse used to be in Titusville but now it's in Viera near Melbourne, about an hour from downtown Orlando. I stopped by a convenience store a few blocks from the courthouse to grab a snack. I heard a voice behind me ask, "Is it too early to buy beer?" I turned around and it was an Orlando attorney with a 12-pack of Coronas to guzzle on the drive back to Orlando at 9:30 a.m. He's not an A-lister and likely doesn't have a heavy client load, so he'll booze it up for the rest of the day. Many attorneys have flexible schedules so the camouflaging of alcoholism is widespread.

A work-a-day, 9-to-5 guy couldn't show up to work smelling like booze. I had a great career and success. But I still went from riches to rags more than once, and all due to alcohol.

CHAPTER 32, SHATTERED SHELLS TO DETOX HELL

Water seeks its own level. My social life and my love life attracted people who would participate in and tolerate my lifestyle. Along with all the erratic, hysterical and insane behavior that came with constant saturation of alcohol, I also managed to get into a very ill-fated marriage in my early 40s. The poor dear could not have been worse for me. We shared a mutual love of alcohol. In AA parlance, when it came to women, my picker was broken.

I vaguely knew her when we were teens, and she also was in the legal world. She assumed if anybody was arrested, they were most certainly guilty. Her favorite hobbies were sleeping and talking to her parents on the phone for hours at a time. We got married basically because the other people our age were getting married. It was time. The brief courtship resulted in a short-term marriage.

It was alcohol-infested ultra-toxic from the get-go. While she also was an alcoholic, it was not palpable to the outside world because my abhorrent behavior was so off the charts that nobody noticed that she too was drunk every night and not functioning well. She held a great job and she could go unnoticed as she worked from home part of the time. She wanted me to be quiet in the mornings so she could sleep. I would often drive by the marital home after my first round of morning appearances to find her in bed asleep well into late mornings. She could easily hide behind layers of government bureaucracy, just not show up, and still get paid. To make matters worse and ultimately really horrific for yours truly, since her pop was a cop, they had close ties to the D.A.s office.

For about two decades at that point, people had attempted many methods to try to get me to stop drinking and to save me from this quick collision course with death. My wife's method would be to call 911 and tell police that I had put my hands on her. This served a number of purposes. They would remove me from the house, arrest me, and then my wife could have some temporary distance from me and my maniacal alcohol-driven behavior.

One day, I was at the end of a particularly severe two-week drinking binge. Sometimes I was too drunk to converse or communicate. At other times, the yelling, screaming, accusing and breaking of furniture, reached an unbearable level. As my wife was preparing to leave the house,

I was begging and cajoling for her to get me a bottle of vodka before she departed. All the bottles in the home were bone dry. I was not functional enough to make it to the liquor store and had run out of options. She flatly refused. She coldly stared at me and informed me she was calling the police and The Florida Bar to report that I was neglecting my clients. This set me into an unbridled frothing fit of rage. I screamed at the top of my lungs that that if she did not get me some booze, I would throw every piece of her property in the street, change the locks on the doors, and let the world know what a drunk she was. She responded by picking up a big round glass of seashells and slammed them to the floor and started screaming, "Get off of me! Get off of me!"

She then ran down the Mexican tile hallway. In my stupor, I was confused. As stupid drunk as I was, I was scratching my head as to what had just taken place. Then, blurry eyed I glanced to the left and noticed the kitchen phone was sitting on the kitchen counter with the receiver off the hook. I picked it up and said, "Hello."

The response was, "Sir, this is 911. Units are on the way."

It was not law, but it was police policy that when a domestic violence call was made, someone was going to jail. The reason was that if law enforcement leaves a violent situation without separating the parties, they can get themselves in hot water later if violence ensues and escalates.

I became one of the falsely accused for domestic violence. I saw the cases pass through the courts all the time where someone scratched their own face on a brick or bruised themselves to fake evidence. Now I was standing with in shock as tables were being turned against me.

Before I could react, three uniformed officers were already at the house pounding on the door, red-faced and ready to click silver bracelets on this criminal defense lawyer. My heart sank. One of the responding officers knew me well. I had taken great pains to harass and embarrass him in front of a jury just a month before, in of all things, a domestic violence trial. The verdict had come back not guilty. He had a great dislike for defense attorneys and me in particular. I was going for the ride this time.

When we got to the County jail, I vaguely remember they were contemplating whether or not to take me to the hospital or to the medical ward of the jail. I don't know how they knew I was in medical distress. I guess my other half had told them, or more likely, it was just that obvious. I could not stand up on my own power anymore. I could not tell them what day of the week it was or even what month. They opted to keep me in jail in the medical wing. The term medical wing has a nice ring to it but it was in reality some version of hell.

Medical in this case consisted of a four-day stay in what is referred to as the Buck Naked Room. It was a solid concrete four-by-six space with a steel bed. It had a small slot in the iron door for purposes of conversing with staff and receiving food. They left me naked in this room that they keep at 60-degrees. I was left in there with nothing but concrete and steel. I had no clothing, no blanket, no pillow, just cold steel.

Occasionally jail staff would peer in through the door to see if I was alive, to laugh at me, and to make humiliating and derogatory comments while I detoxed. The only slightest relief was periodic delivery of medicine which I assume was Benzodiazepines. I shivered. I shook. I begged for a blanket. I begged for water. I begged for a telephone for days. It was basically the mental ward of the county jail. I was so weak from dehydration that I barely had the strength to wrap myself in my own arms to attempt to bring my knees to my chest to try to achieve some warmth. After two days I was able to take a bite of food that was delivered to me from the slot. The glop smelled like dog food.

My brain was scrambled. The most horrific of dreams, nightmares and dark thoughts tortured me further. I was pretty sure I was in hell. Nothing could be worse.

Well, something was worse. I heard the deafening clank of the 5-inch-thick metal door opening and in came Buck Naked psycho number two. A tall athletic black man also naked was forcibly shoved into my small room. I found out later he had attempted to consume paper, paperclips and anything within reach while he was in court for his trial for bank robbery.

Well, this was the end. I was surely going to get the shit beat out of me, raped, and emerge from this hell unrecognizable. God has a way though. It turns out this man was articulate, calm, helpful and was playing the system. He was playing it to act crazy in an attempt at some point to receive a lesser sentence because he had psychiatric issues. Better yet, and miraculously enough, he knew exactly who I was. When a known criminal defense attorney gets locked up, word gets around the jail house pretty quickly. I was a curiosity to him.

He made pretty quick work of making the temperature warmer in the cell. He dampened some toilet paper, folded it into a square and threw it accurately to stick to the air conditioning vent on the ceiling. After about ten minutes, he had engineered a stop to the freezing air flooding into the cell. I was amazed and relieved. I was grateful.

It is impossible to describe the uncomfortable feeling of sitting there with this stranger with everything shriveled up to the size of peas trying to survive this psychiatric nightmare.

When the first round of garbage food got passed through the slot after his arrival, he peeled an orange and handed it to me and insisted I eat it or I was going to die from malnutrition. He gave me his peeled orange as well. He seemed genuinely concerned and treated me like an old friend. While he treated me with respect, whenever the corrections officers would show themselves, he would become abrasive and attempt to become violent towards them. I'm guessing he did this so they would report to the authorities that he was indeed crazy.

Finally, after the Benzos had taken hold, I was led to a shower for the first time in four days. A female officer watched as I stood under the hot water and the first feeling of warmth radiated through every corner and crevice of my body. I could still barely walk due to malnutrition, dehydration and alcohol overdose. My vision was so blurred that I could not see beyond a few feet. I was coming back to life. The shower was a relief like no other. She kept telling me my time was up but I could not move. This simple pleasure of having hot water heat my body was glorious. She finally screamed they would have to remove me if I did not step from the shower. I was escorted to a small vestibule waiting area where they handed me an ill-fitting jumpsuit with "inmate" painted on the back. I was now the property of the County Sherriff's Office. I was also given a pair of jail slides which are plastic shoes with no laces. I was able to take my pick of aged cracked mattresses to be my property during my incarceration.

I was led into an area full of inmates for orientation. There was no available bed space, only slices of unoccupied concrete floors to lay or sit. The echoing concrete walls was ridiculously loud from the yelling, screaming, and fighting of 20 inmates. After a while, an officer in charge came in and gave a lecture of what behavior was expected before we were assigned to a pod. After an indeterminate period of time, either hours or days, my name was called, "Wander, Roll it up!" I dutifully picked up my nasty smelly mattress and followed a corrections officer to my pod. Surely this would be the area where I would have my ass beat and food stolen. I just concentrated as best as I could on how I would get out of this hell. I walked into the dorm-style pod still toxic and weak and was directed to a bunk. The horrific negative and devastating thoughts pervading my consciousness exceeded any horror flick. I shuffled to a cold steel table designed for chow and card games and sat down and laid my head in the corner of my elbow and forearm. I was laying such that my wristband which had my identification number and my name was visible.

As I was half dozing, a voice, not an unfriendly one, said, "Aren't you Jack Wander the lawyer?"

Barely audible, I responded, "Yes."

He snapped, "You're my fucking lawyer and we have court tomorrow."

I just raised my head and looked at him. What could I say? I still hadn't spoken to anyone in the outside world and had no idea what was going on with his case or any part of life in outside of the jail walls. I figured that the world on the other side of the jail was collapsing due to my non-availability. Turns out, the world was somehow surviving without me during this ordeal. This man though, my absence did affect. There began my 30-day odyssey in jail.

From the 30-day jail term, I was driven directly to a substance abuse treatment center in Tampa for 90 days. I went straight there without one day at home. The center was not as regimented as jail. It was considered in-patient. Once again, I found myself in the company of other alcoholics and addicts, mostly athletes, politicians, and other attorneys trying to get their shit together.

I did not go to my house for 120 days while I was in jail and in the treatment center. My wife visited a few times. She also moved out during that time and let my house go to shit.

Prior to the wife's 911 call, I was on a $500 bond. I was already charged with disorderly conduct because I got in a drunken fight at a lounge near where I lived. It's the law that you if you violate your bond you have to stay in jail until the case is settled.

The wife knew this and orchestrated the false allegation with the law listening on the phone. The law was on board because they could cuff this smarmy defense attorney. It was a wet dream for them. She wanted the key turned, for me to lose my law license, and watch my life completely fall apart.

We went from love-hate to hate-hate shortly after wedding bells. We didn't know much about each other and as we learned more over three short years, we found quickly that we only had drinking in common. Naturally with all of this controversy, we got divorced. We had no child support or alimony for a short-term marriage. It was unremarkable as divorces go. It just ended.

The drinking, however, did not end. Another AA term is hitting rock bottom which is when a person thinks their behavior has reached a reprehensible level that they just can't sink any lower. Consequences like divorce and jail time could be considered rock bottom. Not for Jack Wander though. Jack learned zero. As soon as I got the treatment gurus off of my back and appeared to be functioning, I commenced to drinking heavily again. I could not remain sober.

CHAPTER 33, DOUBLE LIFE TROUBLE

In my early 40s I was again leading a double life. I was at the end stage of chronic alcoholism. If I was abstinent for a few months and decided to have a few beers after golf, it would always head to the same place. I would soon be comatose on the floor with a bottle of vodka next to me. My friends and family had pretty much given up on me.

On the flip side of this double life, somehow, I was also owning and operating an insanely successful law practice. I had several layers of enablers around me who would cover for me when I was in a stupor. I had a trial in two weeks defending a physician who had been accused of physically attacking his wife. I had to be clean, sober and on-point in two short weeks

I had to detox from alcohol again. I took a slug off the vodka to achieve a moment of calm so I could plan. I had been to detox and rehab countless times. I couldn't bear the thought of checking into the hospital again with paper slippers and cups of Benzos to bring me down from my toxic state. Like other alcoholics, I wanted to "wean" myself off of the booze instead of the cold turkey method. The problem with that was that the weaning process often turned into another blackout drunk situation.

It was Thursday afternoon and my books were cleared until Monday morning. I chugged four shots of vodka and threw the empty bottle of Belvedere into the wooded side yard. It was a graveyard of empty vodka bottles. Whoever moved into that house after me probably dug it all up and asked themselves, "What fucked up tribe lived here?"

The neighborhood was idyllic. The house was situated in the middle of the third oldest golf course in the state of Florida, Rolling Hills. Parts of the golf course had small hills like in North Georgia or North Carolina. Rolling Hills was built in 1926 for Mobsters from Chicago who flew into nearby private airports, played golf for the weekend, and flew out again. During World War II it was converted to a cow pasture for food to help with the war effort. Many Florida golf courses during the war were used for farmland. The course re-opened in the 1940s. My house was on a wooded acre lot surrounded by similar homes and landscapes.

In my comfortable house, the uncomfortable white-knuckle, gut-wrenching detox process had started with profuse sweating. For two nights I had no sleep, only vomiting, diarrhea and the most hideous thoughts.

I worried, "I'll lose my law business. I won't be able to see my family. I'll be committed to an asylum. I'll die."

After 48 hours or so the indescribable craving for alcohol had subsided. I was able to take small sips of water or ginger ale without being nauseous. I was able to communicate some with the outside world and conduct a little bit of business.

As I walked through the home, I saw the home across the street through the window. I noticed a girl in a bikini looking at me from inside the other home. I averted my eyes but every time I walked past the window, she was still standing there. She was attractive and looked about 30 or so. I was starting to get unnerved by her presence. I wondered why she was staring at me. So, I walked to my mailbox to see if I could tell who it was. When I walked down the driveway, I realized the girl was not there.

Back in the house I made a business call or two. As I talked to a prosecutor about a case coming to trial, I peered out of the back window. Through the trees, I saw several groups of well-dressed people walking through the backyard of the neighbor behind me. I mentioned to the lawyer on the line that there must be an estate sale because people are milling around. I ended the call so I could go outside to see what the people were doing. I walked from the back door to talk to the old folks but there was nobody there. In fact, I was beginning to hallucinate from the alcohol withdrawal.

Throughout the day, a myriad of people stopped around the house. It started with Incan Indians from the 1400s, early American settlers from the 1800s, and all different eras, like flipping channels of a TV. The characters did not come near me. I was terrified but I knew on some level that they were hallucinations. The closest that any of the visions came to me was an elderly black woman wearing a bonnet who sat on the back porch for a while. I watched the alcohol-induced parade of people throughout the night.

I felt like I was dying or having a dark spiritual experience. Within the next 36 hours I felt human again and functional enough to go back into the world. A horrific experience like that kept me away from alcohol in the coming weeks. The thought or scent of vodka made me queasy. The next weeks were filled with maniacally trying to put affairs in order. I also had to see if there had been any really bad public relations for me from the last drinking spree so I could do damage control. It was time to dive into the flip side of my double life.

It was a violent horrible downward cycle. Non-alcoholics can't possibly understand. Friends and family would tell me, "Just stop." It's not that easy. It's definitely not easy. My double life held me in a double-fisted stronghold. I moved from my cushy golf house to a condo. My addictions moved with me.

CHAPTER 34, MAKE IT A DOUBLE

I was out cold on my condo tile floor. I came into consciousness with law enforcement and ambulance personnel breaking through my door. A family member had called 911 for a well-being check since nobody had heard from me for several days. I was sprawled on the kitchen floor with a half empty bottle of vodka on either side of me. My hip was dislocated, which was a very serious injury that would only be caused by a traumatic event with significant torque and force. To dislocate a human hip would take something like a highspeed collision. I had no recollection of any traumatic event or injuring my hip. I was in a blackout for God knows how long with no food, no water, but just me and my vodka as far as I knew.

The rescue team hoisted me on a gurney and rushed me to the local hospital. It took four men and an orthopedic surgeon to hold me down and hoist my hip back into place. There was no way to tell how long the hip joint had gone without its necessary flow of blood and nutrients. I was lucky I was rescued.

I was later told by family and hospital staffers that I continued to reek of alcohol for days after the stint at the hospital. The doctors sent me packing with a handful of prescriptions for pain pills and benzos and the like. That was really bad foresight on their part. By this point in my life the only people that I could persuade to get me booze and prescription drugs were folks equally as ill as I was, or worse yet, clients who wanted to do their attorney a solid. Enablers encircled me.

Since my condo was on the second floor, it was an ordeal to get up the stairs on crutches. I managed with my horrific injury. I made the best of my limited mobility. With the fresh supply of Vicodin and Xanax and other prescriptions, I ordered up more booze and the party continued for a month.

I was sick. I was tired. I was dwindling away in every respect. A friend was checking on me every now and then to make sure I wasn't dead. I wasn't dead yet. I wasn't truly living either. I was listening to the same CDs of my favorite music over and over again and becoming increasingly melancholy.

I read and re-read memoirs written by other drunks. In particular, I loved the book "Dry" by author Augusten Burroughs. I liked his writing style, but moreover, I totally related to his experience. He was a high-paid advertising exec who stayed out partying till wee hours then had to maintain during the day to be successful under his cohorts' scowls and enabling. I loved his description of rehab. I bit right into it. I read it because it was like a security blanket for me to know I wasn't totally alone in the world of end stage addiction. Mr. Burroughs had been in my same insane world.

Somehow, the friend that was checking on me, tracked down Mr. Burroughs and explained my plight. It was reported back to me from his staff that his response was, "If he's not ready, he is not ready," meaning that I had to find my own alcoholic bottom.

It was impossible to engage in this destructive behavior and not have the world notice. A big part of my world was The Florida Bar and they again caught wind of my aberrant behavior. I conducted my business over the phone and convinced other trusted attorneys to continue to make court appearances on my behalf for my clients. Somehow, through manipulation of other lawyers and getting on the phone frequently with clients, I kept my practice squeaky clean. I never took a dime inappropriately. I never was accused of being incompetent by any clients. I was totally obsessive – compulsive about making sure clients were accounted for and every legal obligation to them was fulfilled. From my clients' point of view, my practice was Stirling. That façade was becoming more and more difficult to maintain and conceal the underlying reality of my sickness. I was leading a double life. My personal life was an alcohol and drug-induced train wreck. My personal lunacy was becoming exposed and caused concern by The Florida Bar that I could screw up people's fates, fortunes or lives unless some action was taken. Deep in my subconscious, I knew if I wanted to maintain my law license, I needed to act decisively and rapidly.

So, I went to another round of rehab. It was time to go to detox or make some bolder move. Somehow in my fog, I arranged a bed at Sierra Tucson in Tucson, Arizona. For the price of $40,000, I would detox over 30 days at what is considered to be one of the most luxurious treatment centers. The day came for me to depart for Arizona and some kind soul who was making sure I wasn't dead yet drove me to the airport. I drank the whole way there. We both knew there was a very slim chance that I would make it through security or onto the airplane in my drunken condition. To my amazement, I did. On the flight itself I was seated in the midst of a well-known rugby team. They had just finished a tournament at Disney Sports. What a stroke of luck! These guys were so young, drunk, loud, handsome and rowdy that I was not the least bit noticeable. Plus, they readily shoved beer and shots my way without a second thought. The flight went smoothly with Team Booze.

I staggered to the baggage carousel and in double vision saw a man holding a sign that said "Jack Wander." He nodded that he recognized me. I assume he was shown photos of incoming guests like me for the reason he should, we might be drunk and incoherent. We might also waiver and not commit to rehab and run off with a rugby team to party. He mercifully picked up my one piece of luggage and put me in a wheelchair to transport me to his car. I was obliterated drunk. I could feel other travelers staring at me with disdain.

Sierra Tucson was heavenly for detox. It was worth the hefty price tag to be chemically sedated and treated gently in very clean and comfortable surroundings. The staff was spot-on prompt, courteous and helpful. After four days in the medical wing, I was assigned a room in the lodge for the treatment to begin. My roommate was a high-profile professional baseball player who had gotten too many DUIs and was doing 45 days in this luxurious facility in lieu of a stinky jail. Next door were two professional musicians from different bands. Each of the bands had Top Ten Albums playing on the radio at the time of our mutual stint in ritzy rehab. Other high-profile types ended up in Sierra during my time there.

For the first time, rehab blew by and I didn't want to leave! In this facility they did not prevent men and women from intermingling. In most rehabs they separate the opposite sexes. When folks sober up and get some nutrition in them, then crazy things start to happen. We alcoholics can be manipulative and self-absorbed. So, feeling so far from the comforts of home, men and women tend to look to each other for comfort and affirmation.

Sierra kept you on schedule during the day with individual and group sessions and recreation. Normally in rehab settings, patients are taken by the staff to local AA meetings in the community. Sierra was remotely located so nighttime was spent at in-house AA meetings. This also made it more private for the celebrities there. We had karaoke parties, movies and other planned activities then patients were free to roam the spacious campus under the Arizona desert sky until 10 p.m. A lot of hookups and other fun took place during those hours beside a cactus, behind the stables, or wherever.

I got to know people's lives, dreams, demons, secrets and most everything about them in these rehab settings. There was an exit ceremony with singing and chanting. Each of us were presented with a coin symbolic of our sobriety and our commitment to stay sober. Sierra had an additional part of the ceremony celebrating sobriety. We each made a note, crumpled the paper, announced to the group what we were giving up and then threw the paper ball into the raging firepit. I announced that there would be no more drunk dialing in my future.

As is typical of rehab graduations, patients assure everyone that they will remain sober and keep in touch. During my stay I had become close to a Beverly Hills Realtor. Sure enough, we started dating long distance between Florida and California and, sure enough, inadvisably we started drinking together. She drank exactly like I did, meaning to extreme excess. Mistake Numero Uno was to invite this mirror image, Miss Double Trouble, into my double life.

As a rule of thumb in recovery, you are not supposed to make any major changes in your life in the first year. Long distance dating from both the west and east coast of the U.S. would fall into this category. Nonetheless, my deviant inner compass led me to rack up frequent flyer miles visiting Miss Double Trouble in L.A. I fell in love with that part of the world. I would stay there for weeks at a time with surfboard in tow. I got to know So-Cal with the locals drinking alcohol with my new friend.

One of the people I met through Miss Double Trouble in hoity-toity Beverly Hills was her mother. She was very smart and involved in her daughter's life and sized me up quickly and rendered that Jack was really bad news. She promptly bought me a plane ticket to Orlando and put me in a cab headed for the airport. Well, forget that! I was in California. I had cash and I had no commitments in front of me. I didn't make the flight she had arranged. I did wake up in Longwood two weeks later. I was intact and uninjured but completely clueless where the previous two weeks had gone. I pieced together that I had frequented the La Brea liquor store a number of times after leaving Beverly Hills. Then, it appears from credit card receipts that I spent several days in Malibu in a hotel. I had my wallet and cash in my pockets so nobody rolled me. I had no idea how I made it back to Florida. I had a vodka bottle next to me. The one vague recollection I did have was that I had convinced the cabbie on the way to my home to stop for liquor.

Rehab clearly did not work. Things were getting dicey now. I literally was losing weeks of my life. I had fessed up to the legal world that I was going to rehab so I had a pass for a while. It was a bold and brave step because they were tracking my moves. The numbers were not in my favor. This was the tenth rehab and the first time I blacked out for multiple weeks. My law license was hanging by a thread. People said when I was in complete blackout I could remember case names and dates and details. So, I could appear to function. That really scared me. The Bar was nipping at my heels even though there were no complaints against me.

Ultimately The Bar thought the public would not be protected if I was allowed to remain in practice. The Bar vs. Jack Wander resulted in the strong suggestion from The Bar bigwigs that I relinquish the privilege to practice law with a fancy phrase called "going inactive not related to misconduct."

My clients were exceedingly happy, the court personnel liked me, and The Bar could not pinpoint any acts of incompetence, unethical behavior, or taking money or property. They just seemed to want me out of practice. I was, after all, a known drunk. I'd get cleaned up just in time to escape trouble. I frustrated the bureaucrats because they couldn't quite get ahold of me.

I reluctantly relented. My own disinterested attorney and figure heads from The Florida Bar assured me if I got sober I'd be practicing law again in a year. I already knew all too well The Bar and the Supreme Court of Florida's tendencies to be particularly tough on attorneys with legal issues, which I experienced the first time I went inactive when I got popped for coke.

A point of interest is the degree of punishment given by the Florida Supreme Court against attorneys with alleged behavior reflecting poorly upon the profession depends largely upon the makeup of the Court at the time of the alleged wrongdoing. If the makeup is ultra conservative an attorney could easily get a long suspension or disbarment. A more left-leaning group of decision makers reviewing the identical conduct might offer an admonishment or symbolic slap on the wrist. The Florida Supreme Court seems to rarely set their sights on well insulated big law firms. They tend to hunt for the street level mavericks who are on the frontline of legal wars daily.

This maverick attorney agreed to give up practicing law for a second time for an estimated year. It sounded doable, but the system is intricate and slow moving to get through legal check points. So, Thanksgiving Day that year, for nearly four agonizing years, I "voluntarily" turned in my law license as a state of inactive. In exchange The Florida Bar was not going to otherwise attempt to suspend my right to practice law or consider disbarment proceedings. I was in pain and angry. I was incensed and distraught. I was lost. I was now going to have to plan for how to live my life until my career was back on track.

CHAPTER 35, FOR THE PEOPLE

The people around me thought it best to give up my law license for a second time. For these people, I gave in to the pressure. With that supposed voluntary action, I lost the income stream from my law practice for four long years.

While my nature is to be a conservative spender, I had spent with wild abandon during the previous few years. I had spent ridiculous amounts of money in my blackouts. I would wake up and have a new luxury sports car in my driveway. A new stereo would be blaring. A trip would be booked. I don't come from big money. In my mid-career, I was earning money, and a lot of it. I had extra cash to spend, so I indulged during this time. With my dramatic shift in income, I powered down the excessive spending spree to live within my means as an inactive lawyer.

Surviving comfortably during the four years, however, was no problem. I had no pain and suffering at all. The people around me wanted to see me suffer. Somehow, they equated hard life circumstances to healing and changing. I didn't agree. The Bar bigwigs, my family and friends, all wanted me to show I was supporting myself and working hard.

Weasel D asked, "How are you surviving? It's a head scratcher Dude." All of my friends were curious of my seeming penny-pinching predicament and yet I was in all respects secure and stable.

I had to show income on paper so I worked part time odd jobs. I did research for other lawyers.

Shockingly to me during the waiting period to get my law license back, The Bar said I could conduct mediations. It looked good to The Bar that I was still involved in law. I took a 40-hour mediation course, then opened shop as a Certified Mediator. Jack Wander the referee listened patiently to warring litigants then urged them towards a resolution so they could lay down their swords. I hated being a referee. I listened to one side and their woes, then the other side about their woes, then tried to find a solution, which usually resulted in each person giving in a little but leaving unhappy. Halfway through the mediations, I'd get impatient. I wanted to be a litigator, not a neutral party, but to pick a side. I'd much rather be the fighter in the ring slugging it out or the warrior in full battle.

I also had two condos in New Smyrna Beach that I rented for income. I did landscaping, or just about anything to earn a few bucks. I needed to show income and some semblance of a respectable life.

It was a tight rope. People were curious about me. People asked a lot of questions. A lot of the people asking the questions suffered from schatenfreude. They enjoyed digging into my humiliation and misfortune. This element tried to conceal their ulterior motives of self-satisfaction and the power of dirt to dish to their gossip circles. They would come on strong with sadness or empathy at my latest implosion and ask if there was anything they could do. These were not true friends but nosey acquaintances just lusting for juicy tidbits previously undisclosed so they could spread new rumors, despite their false assurances of confidentiality.

On the other hand, my lifelong true friends would talk to me about the Gators, my family or surfing and wait to see if I had anything I wanted to unload on them. These people knew me. They knew their continued presence in my life and obvious loyalty was all I needed. I didn't need to unload anymore baggage and they did not care to receive it. I did trust them if I did want to talk. What I did disclose to my inner circle during this gloomy time, I knew would never see the light of day.

People were asking but I wasn't telling, not all anyway. In my vagabond, ex-patriot, dope-dealing days prior to becoming a barrister, I had bought up nooks and crannies in paradise throughout St. Thomas and the Caribbean. While I was running dope decades earlier, I had cash, cash and more cash. I had piles of paper currency stacked up in safety deposit boxes at Banco Popular in St. Thomas. So, I'd buy a quarter-acre here and a half-acre there in St. Thomas and other U.S. currency-friendly islands. Offshore banking and dealing in Caribbean real estate transactions was simple in the 1980s and not highly regulated. So, I bought up real estate lots and I was now unloading the properties from ill-gotten gains from decades earlier.

I had a healthy dose of paranoia, even though confidentially lawyers had told me my investments had no illegal implications after so many years. I kept my income source hush-hush. I was cash rich but had to appear piss poor. For the people, I had to look the part of someone getting punished.

I managed but it sucked. A part of me was missing. I was in agonizing pain every day not practicing law.

CHAPTER 36, THE ABCs OF DEFERRING DETOX

For all of the people in my life, including myself, I wanted desperately to be sober. For the next few years Jack Wander's personal mission statement was clear but not so easy to attain. I had to get sober, stay sober, support myself, and get my law license back. I was like a Jack-in-the-box; try to be dry and get drunk, try to be dry and get drunk. I could not stop drinking for more than a day or two. Every fiber of my being wanted alcohol.

Every drunk has stories about people trying to save them. Periodically friends and family would try to babysit me from the vodka villain. Caring people would pass me around to shield me from "the drunk."

One such attempt during my chronic double life era, The Boxer was getting separated and divorced. He had temporarily moved back into his parents' home where he lived when we were friends in our teens. The Boxer asked me to go to a Magic basketball game at the Orlando arena. While detoxing, the last thing I wanted was to be faced with bright lights, loud noise, and worst of all, having to socialize. I reluctantly agreed to go and stopped by his parents' house to ride together. While he was getting his things together to stay at my house for a few days, I found a bottle of vodka in the kitchen cupboard. I turned up the bottle. That is what we alcoholics do, we drink. He was so innocent about alcoholism, he did not realize he put me into temptation. He didn't realize I would sniff out alcohol anywhere. How could he possibly know that he could not turn his back on me for mere minutes?

The game was stimulating and social, made tolerable by my slugs at the house. Now I was Jonesing again by the end of the game. We drove back to my house so he could babysit me there. I was craving a drink like crazy as we drove the half hour from the downtown Orlando arena to home. A Gator basketball game was on TV so we agreed to watch the game. I told him I was tired and went to my room. I locked the door, opened the sliding glass door to the back yard. My well-meaning friend could not help me. No obstacle course could stop me. Nothing could stop me. I ran to the ABC Liquor Store and ran back. To satisfy my incurable cravings, I could outsmart, outrun, outmaneuver any obstacle. I would find booze like a bloodhound. ABC was mecca. In ten minutes, I was back in my room gulping my coveted vodka. In the second quarter of the game, I was back out in my living room watching the Gators with my buddy like nothing had happened. Something had happened, something bad. He did not know. The Gators were winning. I clearly was losing.

This well-intentioned and caring supervision was frequent in my dark days of detoxing then falling prey to my addiction again and again. My dearest friends would play keep-the-bottle-from Jack and tie me up with surf leashes. They would pour out my booze. During alcohol detox, they should not have poured out the alcohol and send the alkie on the road. They did not understand addiction. Friends mistakenly thought I just wanted to be a good time Charlie, but addiction had a grip on me. My addiction was a physical body phenomenon, like how could I explain an orgasm or a sneeze or extreme hunger? While detoxing, I would have heart pain, heart palpitations, hallucinations, nausea, paranoia, and a host of horrifying sensations. Not only was it hard to explain, it was embarrassing.

Most of my lifelong friends were not alcoholics, so they thought my behavior was pure madness. Many thought I just wanted to be drunk all the time. This phenomenon of around the clock drinking was not what a non-alcoholic thought of as drinking. The word drunk to my friends evoked a mental vision of someone having a good time who is unnaturally happy and giddy. So, my friends and family often got angry with me thinking I was self-indulgent. From the inside looking out, my alcoholism was self-destructive, not self-indulgent. When I got to the stage of daily all-day drinking, there was zero fun or social lubrication involved. It was survival to make every effort to keep the blood alcohol level high enough to function. This level of alcohol toxicity can only lead to jails, institutions or death as I learned in AA. I ended up in both jails and institutions more than once. Death I have managed to defy to date.

CHAPTER 37, ALOHA TO DRINKING

My friend The Boxer eventually gave up on me. My friends weren't calling anymore. I was involved in multiple acts of violence and drunken episodes. I had been in and out of rehab many times. People who had been around me my whole life, not just The Boxer, had given up on me. My closest friends were frustrated and angry at me. After a couple of hours of yet another discussion about my inexplicable craving for vodka, The Boxer had heard enough of my bullshit and exclaimed, "You're such a pansy. Why don't you quit killing yourself slowly and making everyone watch ... why don't you just get a gun and get it over with?"

When we hung up our phones, I thought hard about that statement. The Boxer was right. My life had gone so far off course and I was continuing to deteriorate and crumble. I was unable to pursue my chosen profession since my law license was inactive, my family life had tanked to horrific and then to non-existent, and my friends were frazzled and avoiding me. I made the decision to take The Boxer's advice and kill myself. I thought about simply walking out in front of a large speeding truck on Interstate 4, but I was physically unable to walk more than a few steps because of my lethal alcohol level. I had a vision of my last surf trip in my mind. I couldn't surf. I couldn't even walk. I decided to die in Hawaii, a place I had loved. I booked a flight. I figured I would be fit enough to get on a plane in two days. I packed two bottles of Valium, a plane ticket to Honolulu and a shit-load of cash. I planned to book the most stunning suite on the highest floor with the best panoramic view. When I was ready, I would dump all the pills down my throat and wash them down with an entire bottle of Smirnoff. I was determined to kill myself. I had a plan. I felt at peace as I packed for my last days on earth. I had 48 hours to present myself decent enough to get past the airport security and staff.

I looked miserable. By now, I had not had a drink in 12 hours and I was starting to shake. The heated argument with The Boxer hit me between the eyes. I did not see any options to ending this life. I had been to rehab a ridiculous number of times; I could write a guide book. I got temporarily sober at all of them like Hanley Hazelton, Sierra Tucson, The Beach Comber, Shands-Vista in Gainesville and more and more.

I wanted to end my misery but I had to get through the next handful of hours of life. I decided to reach out one last time for help. On a lark, I reached out to an AA acquaintance and asked where the next Tuesday meeting was. I thought I would give it one last shot. He directed me to a meeting in Winter Park in a church by the railroad tracks.

I was not fit to drive. I was a danger driving to the meeting because I was so toxic and my reflexes were so pitiful. I was frantic and wrought with anxiety. I was slamming on my brakes at yellow lights. I came within inches of cars at stop lights. I used to hide before I went into AA meetings for fear someone of importance would see me. I didn't care anymore. My reputation was of no concern because within the week I would be deceased. I shuffled in reeking of stale booze with bags under my eyes. I was unable to sit still because of the shakes.

On the dicey drive there, I played a game of roulette of sorts in my mind. I prayed. I wasn't typically given to prayer. I prayed that, "If any man approaches me at this meeting to help I will take his help this time and ask him to sponsor me. If not, I'm flying to Hawaii to my final demise."

The hour-long meeting dragged by and I just stared at the floor. I just wanted to go to Hawaii, try to get healthy enough to enjoy the trip some and then kill myself. I was embarrassed. I barely said a word at the meeting. I was shaking so hard that I could not enunciate any actual words when it came my time in the circle to speak. All I could muster was the basics with stuttering, "I'm J-J-J-Jack and I'm an-an-an alcoholic." Now I really had some color in my face of deep red. I was humiliated. After the Lord's Prayer at the end of the meeting, I moved as quickly as I could to the door. I thought I was making tracks but I was later told I was moving at a turtle's pace.

As I was leaving through the church door I felt a hand on my shoulder. A kindly man named Ed strode up to me after the meeting and introduced himself. I managed a staccato slurred, "Will you be my temporary sponsor?"

He said, "No, not temporary, but I will be your sponsor."

CHAPTER 38, FROM A TO ME

My prayer was answered at that AA meeting. I was to live after all. After meeting my new sponsor Ed at the Alcoholics Anonymous meeting, I maneuvered the BMW I bought during a blackout back from Winter Park to my home without a car accident. This was the first miracle.

I had stashed Michelob beers in my closet. I downed the warm beers to stop shaking. I cancelled my flight to Hawaii.

I met Ed every day after that for four weeks. Ed and I dedicated the time to marching through the 12 Steps of AA. God is written all over AA, so people including myself thought it might be too religious or like a cult. I was wrong. I learned the only way people stay sober is by virtue of admitting wrongs and asking forgiveness. In the 12 Steps, I had to first admit powerlessness over alcohol and that my life was unmanageable. Step nine was to make amends but I had to have sobriety behind me first. I looked to my sponsor to tell me when the time was right. Then I was led to help others.

I enjoyed getting to know Ed. He was a retired lawyer. He was a thin man and a harmless, kind human being. He lived for God, family and AA, in that order. He was sober for 30 years and was always looking for newcomers to the program to help them get and stay sober.

About three weeks into the process I was getting ready to go to a noon AA meeting. I looked in the mirror. The whites of my eyes were white and my face muscles and skin on my face eased back into a natural state. My hair had protein in it and was shiny. As I looked in the mirror I felt remarkably different.

For the first time in my adult life the obsession for alcohol had been lifted. Mystically or magically the craving had left my being. The insane urge left me. I got chills and was truly happy for the first time in a very, very long time.

I put on my deserved smile and bounded down the stairs of my condo. Getting into my car, my young adult Asian neighbor gave me a triple-take. This neighbor was weary of me for good reason. I had used every manner of deceit and deception previously on her and her boyfriend to help me acquire alcohol. After a few people in my life had relieved me of my car keys, let air out of my bike tires, confiscated cash and credit cards, I had looked to these poor neighbors as a way to get a fix of booze. I don't know how many times I told them my aunt had died. I'm sure she figured I didn't have 30 aunts. It was all pretty humiliating stuff to now face in my sobriety.

This was a new day following a life-altering four weeks.

She exclaimed from her driveway, "You look like a different person altogether."

With an ear-to-ear smile I responded, "Yes, I feel different. I am different. I have had a bit of an awakening."

Alcohol had taken me from A to Z in the checklist of terrible side effects of addiction. Now Jack was back. I wasn't different at all. I was Jack again. I was the Midwest kickball-playing little kid that had been benched in the game of life for a long, long while.

CHAPTER 39, THE GRIP OF SOBRIETY

I was alive again with a new sobriety and new way of life. Getting sober was a miracle for me. I was in a deep dark alcohol and drug-infested hole for seemingly most of my life. Then all of a sudden, I was on solid ground looking down in the hole and taking a hard look at the years that I spent there.

In the years before the fact of my alcoholism bubbled to the surface and became unavoidably visible, I had managed to surround myself with many capable wonderful people. Friends, family, business colleagues and mental health professionals had tried to save me from myself. If it were possible for others to make me sober, I had a caring and willing cast of characters to do so. Unfortunately for the suffering alcoholic, the answer and the cure only lie within. I found the only way to get and remain sober was to achieve and maintain contact and reliance on a Higher Power. For me, it took dozens of relapses and revisits to the hell of chronic and deadly drinking before I could get better. Once clean and sober for a while, I achieved what AA calls "some walking around sense."

Life as it could be clicked into razor sharp focus. Life was glorious. I was so happy to be truly alive. The deadly desire to drink or drug was gone. I felt powerful that I now recoiled from alcohol. My new sobriety was not just survival, but the commencement or re-commencement of living a complete and beautiful life on life's terms. This meant just because I was sober that things won't always go my way and when they don't, I am not going to drink over it. AA taught me this concept.

My physical being took on a radical healing. It took six months to flush the poisons out of my system. As a big drinker, I had bloat in my mid-section with skinny arms and legs.

With my new look, also came a fresh mental outlook. The most surprising change to me was that I was so strongly attracted to attendance of AA meetings. The 12 Steps of AA worked for me. The odds of survival of a hardcore chronic alcoholic are small. The odds of remaining free of incarceration or being institutionalization are slim, if the alcoholic does survive. The only way out for me was AA and changing life according the dictates of that program. AA showed a road map to living which was ultra-gratifying, especially when I had the opportunity to help pull other alcoholic sufferers out of the mire of sure devastation. I attended at least one meeting every day – voluntarily. I made many lifelong friends in the rooms of AA.

I learned that instead of regretting and obsessing over my past misdeeds, to utilize past as an asset to be used towards living life soberly and spiritually going forward.

My shredded relationships fell back into place with the help of the program. I had the privilege of apologizing and making amends to the many people who I had harmed and disappointed.

The transition from the walking dead to life went smoothly overall. One thing that got uncomfortable was Step 5 where I had to admit to my sponsor Ed the exact nature of my wrongs. I had to admit about the drug running and the income from the island properties. He assured me it was in my past and it was nobody's business.

In previous attempts at sobriety, I had poo-pooed the notion of sponsorship and working the 12 Steps and trusting a Higher Power. Now, I craved all of those things. Instead of judging what others said at meetings and looking for reasons to criticize them, I reacted to every word spoken at the meetings as gold. Every person inspired me. Members of AA speak the same language that only an alcoholic would truly understand. I found it comforting beyond description to the be in the company of fellows who have found their way to a life of happiness, joy and freedom through sobriety.

CHAPTER 40, A FLASHLIGHT ON THE LEGAL SYSTEM

I navigated the four years that my law license was inactive by trying to be positive and purposeful. I called it the Tebow Era. Tebow was my dog. I worked out and concentrated on having healthy relationships with those close to me. I was sober. I was in great shape. I was mostly waiting day-by-day to be an active lawyer again.

Out of the blue, I got a life changing call with great news. I got my law license back for the second time. I was walking on sunshine. I could hardly contain my excitement and feeling of triumph. Within the hour I was putting my practice back together. I was back in the game in no time. I worked hard and business filled my calendar. My operating account started to have a pulse again. So, here I was again navigating poor souls through the criminal justice system.

Cases of interest started to roll in such as Clint. He had everything in life going against him except for one trait I desperately envied, he was handy. He could build, repair, recondition, fabricate and fix anything mechanical. He sold these skills for $20-per-hour. At the time he hired me, he was trading his time for the rehabilitation of a home in Apopka where he was born, raised and currently lived.

The biggest things he had going against him were the facts that he had three baby-mamas after him for child support, the government was after him for back taxes, and he had a crippling meth habit. He looked the part of a meth addict. He was a white guy with scraggly hair, sallow skin, and a general disheveled appearance. He had just been popped with some meth in his work truck.

Clint came to my office on the recommendation of his former boss. Most of my business was from referrals and my former clients were hearing that I was back in business. Word of mouth was the best advertisement for me. I grew up in Florida so that helped because I knew a lot of local people. I got one satisfied customer after the next, then my good name went out to the wind. People had positive experiences and satisfactory results with my firm, then they referred me to their friends. Clint's boss was an example of a former client who sent his employee to a trusted lawyer.

I told Clint I needed $12,000 for me to take his case and that did not include a jury trial. When I made the legal fee quote, Clint looked distraught. I thought he was going to take his pile of papers and sprint out of the office. He sat pensively for a moment. He asked for a few minutes to use his cell phone in the lobby. When he returned he said he would deliver the fee the next day. On his phone, he arranged to take $1,200 out of the bank earmarked for child support arrearage, to borrow $5,000 from his mother, and to sell his restored El Camino Royale for a fraction of the value.

I sometimes felt self-conscious about the amount of money I made. Somehow, successful lawyers were given some peculiar combination of talent and luck. We assessed a situation, researched the circumstances, figured out which legal screws to turn, and searched our brains for favors from legal friends. We finally ran our mouths in a courthouse in front of a judge and that ultimately earned the fees. It seemed obscene to me that we could make so much money at such a fluffy-leather-couch endeavor. On the other hand, guys like Clint were truly working hard physically turning wrenches, installing AC units, tweaking plumbing and electric, and sweating their asses off for his hourly fee. In the end, Clint's hard-earned money was very well spent on his legal defense.

He had been charged with possession of 12 grams of methamphetamine at 2 a.m. on the day in question. Clint had been driving southbound on Highway 441 in Apopka at a time when roads are mostly empty. A cop driving eastbound in a perpendicular street claimed he could tell Clint was driving with high beams on, which is illegal. The Apopka city cop made a U-turn and followed Clint for two miles. Clint did not violate any traffic laws. He was driving an old work truck duly tagged and registered in this small rural town where he caught the attention of a bored dishonest cop. Officer Friendly hit the blue lights just before the jurisdiction went from the Orange County part of Apopka to the Seminole County line in Altamonte Springs.

If the cop waited until Clint got to the Seminole County line, it would have been an invalid or illegal stop and the case could have been beat rather easily by any competent defense lawyer.

In this case, Clint dutifully pulled his Chevy to the side of the road in a safe grassy area. Officer Friendly demanded Clint's license, registration and insurance papers. Clint had the papers ready and repeatedly asked why he had been stopped. He pointed out that he hadn't been speeding, weaving or running any stop lights. The cop would not answer him. The officer was more intent on aggressively searching the interior of Clint's truck with a high-powered flashlight looking for any evidence of criminal wrongdoing. The officer correctly assumed that Clint was not on a job. He also knew that gaunt and nervous look on the face of an addict. Without any hard evidence or illegal behavior, the cop was still on a mission. He ordered Clint out of the truck for a standard standby cop reason – officer safety. Once Clint opened the door to exit the truck, the illegal search of Clint's truck began in earnest. Clint knew his protestations of the cop's behavior would only encourage anger by Officer Friendly but Clint couldn't help himself. He kept asking why he was stopped to begin with and kept telling the cop to stop searching his truck.

Clint did not do anything illegal. The cop, on the other hand, was conducting an illegal search.

The officer responded to Clint's disgruntlement by calling for backup and reported to dispatch that he was searching a vehicle because he observed a crushed soda can and saw white powder on the floorboard of the decade-old construction truck. Once backup arrived for the Apopka city cop, they executed an extreme search of the vehicle. In the right rear passenger seat, the officer found a flashlight which he unscrewed, peered into, and hit the motherload. There was a cellophane bag with 12 grams of meth.

Clint was handcuffed and stuffed into the cop car and taken to the Apopka jail for questioning. He bonded out on $2,000 bail and was given a court date.

Sometimes it was possible for me to resolve a case in a couple of hours. Sometimes I made a call to a prosecutor to work something out or ask for a plea conference, an orchestrated conference with the judge. Sometimes the threat of going to trial resolved the issue. Trials can be expensive and it was best for all involved to find a resolution prior to trial if possible. This was not one of those quick-fix cases.

I eagerly attacked this assignment. In my opinion, there was absolutely no reason to stop Clint on this occasion and absolutely no reason to search his vehicle. The minute the D.A. provided me with the police reports, I filed a motion to suppress the stop and the search of his vehicle.

This was the United States. We had laws. Cops were not supposed to stop, search, harass, cajole, impede or generally restrict movements of citizens without probable cause. This was the type of situation where blood boils in the veins of true believers and defenders of the U.S. Constitution.

I filed a short ten-page motion to have the evidence thrown out and have the case dismissed. I then arranged for a two-hour hearing in front the presiding judge. Officer Friendly showed up all buttoned-up, shined-up and ready to B.S. his way through the hearing. He claimed he could tell Clint's high beams were on even though his view of the vehicle was from the side and he never saw the lights straight on. When asked on cross examination if he had any training or experience to discern whether or not a vehicle had high beams activated from the side of a vehicle, he said yes. He gave the judge a contrived detailed explanation of such training. I, as defense counsel, moved to invalidate the stop and have the case thrown out and ended. I quoted legal precedent that stated that if law enforcement could detect such things from that sort of vantage point, then they should be working for NASA rather than local law enforcement. The judge denied my motion to invalidate the stop on those grounds.

The next inquiry was for the search of the truck. The officer outlined his vast experience at detecting people who were drug users and again noted the crushed soda can which he knew to be used to smoke drugs. Along with his observations of the white powder on the floorboard of the truck, he testified to the judge that the dust looked like cocaine. He further testified that since he had found dope in flashlights before, that justified that he was prompted to open the flashlight.

I did not believe a word of his testimony. I asked the cop if he used the on-scene drug testing equipment for the presence of dope. He said he declined to test before searching further because of exigent circumstances. This is a buzz word used by law enforcement so they can circumvent the Constitution and search if they want to, regardless of a citizen's rights. The theory being that if results from the drug test came up negative, Clint might be able to drive off with narcotics still being somewhere in the vehicle.

I made certain observations of witnesses on the witness stand. I noticed the officer both paused and turned slightly red when asked how many times he had found dope in a flashlight in his tenure as a cop with the Apopka police department. When I asked him on cross examination exactly how many times he found illicit materials in flashlights, he did not have a precise number, but estimated at least a dozen. The word "bullshit" flashed in my mind repeatedly. I could barely contain myself to not yell the word audibly.

The court made its ruling. The judge said, "Based on the officer's extensive experience at discerning from a distance of a side view whether a vehicle had high beams activated, I find that the stop was valid. Additionally, based on the officer's training and experience as an Apopka police officer in discovering narcotics in closed flashlights, I hereby deny the motion to suppress the evidence. This case will go forward to trial."

I was hot. I was incensed. I knew this cop was lying. I quickly devised a plan of action. Defense attorneys were snipers as it related to exploiting the nuances of the Constitution, especially as it related to the Fourth Amendment, the right to be free from unreasonable search and seizures. We had an arsenal of motions to exclude evidence based on details of these Fourth Amendment rights. When prosecutors were up against obviously guilty defendants and they were nullified or terminated because of these loopholes, good citizens got pissed off. Sometimes victims of crimes didn't see justice because of a detail such as Miranda Rights were not read to perpetrators, so the confessions got thrown out of court. Defense lawyers, the conduits to enforce the Constitution, sometimes ended up looking pretty darn slimy to average citizens. Generally, citizens do not like when lawyers exploit loopholes to beat back charges against defendants. In this case, Clint deserved to have his illegal search rectified. I put one of my bullets in my sniper's gun. Thank the Lord and the law there is an avenue for information called the public records request.

As Clint and I parted company, I told him we weren't finished. While it was fresh in my mind, I sprinted four blocks to my office full of venom and adrenaline. I drafted a public records request aimed at the Apopka Police Department requesting every single arrest affidavit of Officer Friendly wherein he made an arrest for drugs or narcotics.

In three days, an older gentleman in the records department called me. He informed me this was an odd request and completing it would be cumbersome, time consuming and expensive. I told him in kindest terms I didn't give a crap. In two weeks, the records were ready. I cleared my afternoon, piled into my Ford 150 and blazed to Apopka City Hall. I forked over a check for $378 for copies and loaded a pile of papers in my banker's box and headed back to my Orlando office. I poured over each arrest affidavit of Officer Friendly since his date of employment at the City of Apopka. In the hundreds of pages related to drug arrests made by this cop, there was not one mention of dope ever being found in or near any flashlight.

My heart was pumping. I drafted a motion for a re-hearing on the motion to suppress. I ordered the transcripts from the hearing and had it typed. Yes, the judge had opined that since the officer found dope many times in flashlights that the case would not be thrown out of court. Armed with a copy of the judge's ruling, along with a compilation of all this cop's drug arrests, we marched back into re-hearing on the appointed day six weeks later.

Not to my surprise, Officer Friendly was nowhere in sight. He wasn't all buttoned up and shined up in his uniform ready to smile at the judge and to brag about what an awesome cop he was this time.

For dramatic effect in what we lawyers refer to as demonstrative aids, I placed the stack of arrest affidavits to my left. In making my arguments to the judge, I argued, "To my left sir, and to your right, at the table of the defense counsel, I give to you all of the drug arrests made by Officer Friendly during his career in Apopka. To my right, Your Honor, is the stack of arrest affidavits where this officer found contraband in or around a flashlight. You will note not one sheet of paper in this pile. Sir, at a minimum, this officer mis-remembered gravely what he had done in his career or he lied to this Court to get a conviction. I am asking you now to reconsider the motion to suppress and to prevent The State from presenting any of the illegally obtained evidence in any further proceeding."

The humbled prosecutor struggled for something to counter. He weakly referenced the idea that the law enforcement officer may have been confused, but since the dope was found it should be used in a trial anyway. The judge would have none of it. He was evidently as red-faced as the state attorney but for different reasons. He was angered that he had been lied to by the cop. The State filed a dismissal that day.

Clint was poker faced. He truly didn't know what I was up to because he was not sophisticated to the language, customs and procedures of courtroom drama that he had just witnessed. He was so glassy-eyed and sweaty that I knew he hadn't stopped using meth. He shook my hand as we parted company on the 12th floor of the courthouse. His hand had the sandpaper texture of a working man and the cold and sweaty nature of an addict.

Despite what may be called a victory in the State of Florida versus Clint, his troubles were far from ending. Since he had magically come up with the money to pay me, he had fallen further behind in his child support. The Department of Revenue, which is the child support enforcement agency in the State of Florida, was on his ass. He had a hearing the following week in the same courthouse for contempt proceedings. If he could not come up with $7,500 for back child support, he was looking at six months in the Orange County Jail. For that case he had a court appointed lawyer, one provided by The State, whom he talked to one time for a total of two minutes, he had told me. Clint was lost in the quicksand of The System – one horrific sinking situation after the next.

The next morning, I received a call from Clint's former boss, the man who referred him to me, to inform me that Clint had died of an overdose of heroin that night. He thought his overdose was intentional.

The case, the story, the saga, or however one would reference the situation with Clint was fairly commonplace during the early 2000s. Experienced defense attorneys lived through story after story about clients like Clint. Some clients just had the cards stacked against them where cops often misrepresented facts, then judges rubber-stamped the declarations and representations of these same law enforcement officers. The system of murky legal proceedings was maddening.

This is not to say that my clients were all innocent or all wronged by the system. There just seems to have developed an us-against-them mentality or a win-at-all-costs mentality in the legal world. Even before law school, as a normal citizen, I pretty much thought people accused of crimes were guilty and needed to be punished. I discovered it was so much more layered and complicated.

True, in Clint's case, those were his illegal drugs. The debate and the dispute raging in courtrooms in every city, in every county, in every state, was how much power were we to give the government and law enforcement over the conduct of our everyday lives.

People at cocktail parties or social events made remarks like, "Your client had these dangerous drugs on him so he deserved to be punished."

I then would either nod politely or try to explain the nuances of the Fourth Amendment.

I would explain the consequences, "This is not Nazi Germany. This is not a land of fascism. We can't let unlawful search and seizures happen unless we want to give up our freedom. In every courtroom every day there are criminal defense types that are trying to defend the liberties of everyone, even and especially the 'Clints' of the world."

I have handled thousands of cases. It was always hard for me to answer the social question, "Are you handling any interesting cases?" They were all interesting to me. Since many criminal cases were in public records, publicly known facts could be discussed without it being attorney-client privilege.

This case was poignant because the judge was so pissed that he had been lied to by the cop. Both Clint and Justice got what they paid for because I took the trouble to uncover the truth of the situation.

To go through the extra machinations was because I was caught up in my world of wanting truth in matters. I wanted to do my part to convey that cops and the government can't have all the power and shouldn't tell us citizens what we can do in our own private cars and own private homes. In piddly-little cases, liberties were being lost thus chipping away at our freedoms. It was easy for the cops to illegally bully citizens because typically nobody was paying attention in a small dope case. In the end, the cop was right, the accused was a drug addict and he overdosed. Nonetheless, for freedom and democracy to work properly, you had to in this case, and in every case, to go through the legal process with integrity.

CHAPTER 41, TRYING TO SKIRT THE LAW

Sometimes cops lie and sometimes witnesses lie. I hate technology. I hate computers. Sometimes though, I have to admit, that digital evidence can benefit a case in unearthing the truth.

Tex was referred from a prior client. He was a scrappy guy with a history of small crimes of violence with instances like battery and bar fights. Despite his relative minor contact with the criminal justice system, he held a responsible and high paying job in the restaurant equipment industry. On the evening in question, Tex was bouncing around the upscale Lake Mary bar scene between Dexter's, Amore and Graffiti Junction. He showed up at my office accused of fondling a girl under her skirt and grabbing her by the throat when she took exception to it.

Tex swore there was no way this shit went down. He said everyone was drinking and socializing at the bar and the girl did not like something he said. His version was the girl was hammered and she started yelling and screaming and it was she who struck him in the neck. Her male friends told Tex to take it outside, which he did, and whipped their asses. They got the worst of the fight. They called the cops and gave four sworn statements that said Tex fondled and grabbed the girl.

Despite the sworn statements, Tex said it was bullshit and he wasn't taking a plea deal from The State because he was innocent.

As is my protocol, I gathered a fee, then immediately sent an investigator to the restaurant to get the surveillance video of the evening of the event. You have to get the video to preserve the evidence before it's destroyed. The restaurant management said they had to go through their corporate office to get the video and they gave some vague assurances they would provide it without a subpoena. Meanwhile, I questioned the female victim under oath with a court reporter present. Two days before the deposition, I got the video footage. It was boring at first. Then the action started. I found it fascinating to watch the behavior of humans at a bar. They arrived sober with conservative body language and were cautious where their eyes went. After a few drinks, people started touching each other and conviviality increased. My client was near the female who was talking to a guy. Tex walked up and spoke to her. There's no audio in the recorded video so I did not know what was said. She approached Tex, slapped him and grabbed him by the throat, and he put his hands in the air. Her male friends came to the rescue, caused a scene, then went outside. Tex was bounced from the bar by management. What is most startling, is the girl did not have on a skirt, she had on jeans.

It was mind-blowing the coordinated embellished lies these people told with their mob-mentality. Now they were stuck with their stories. It is a crime to give a false sworn statement to police. With the video, they couldn't continue to lie. Before surveillance video, you would have to talk to witness upon witness to try to get an honest version of events in cases like this where the facts do not match. This video clearly showed the exact opposite of what the girl described under oath that happened at her watering hole. She was in trouble.

In the deposition, I had an audio-visual technician to run the video player. Before we ran the footage, I went through discovery phase of the deposition and put the girl through the paces. I asked her background information, biography stuff, what she was doing leading up to the time in question, and confirmed her denim skirt and white top.

I asked her, "So, you still take the position of your statement about what happened? Tex put his hand up your skirt and was kicked out of the bar. You realize you are under oath under the penalty of perjury, right?"

The prosecutor was getting indignant.

I gave a pregnant pause and a cold stare, which is in the arsenal of every defense attorney.

Then I asked, "Why did you tell a bold-face lie?"

With that there was an eruption and gnashing of teeth.

I motioned for the technician to put up one frame with a date stamp of Tex in the bar and the girl wearing not a skirt, but jeans. I saw the alleged victim's heart sink. By now she was gulping and sweating and turning red. By virtue of the video, I ripped her to shreds. The only part of her story that was truthful was that Tex was asked to leave the bar.

I often wondered how many innocent people were wrongfully charged by a witness like this without digital evidence to clear their good name. She was well educated, had a professional career and was a credible witness, but she was lying, or at least had a pitiful memory.

The house of cards that was The State's case was folding and the other witnesses came in sheepish and sweating. I asked each one of them why they were liars. That language doesn't fly well with the prosecutors so now I was the bad guy because I pissed off everyone in the room except my client. The case was dismissed. Before technology, my client would have been screwed.

Attorneys today may not have video evidence for each case, but they are armed with the knowledge that people embellish and make shit up. This group rallied in the cause of prosecuting Tex. They obviously would say or do anything to push that cause. It happens all the time in American courts.

Before all the big brother eavesdropping, defense lawyers had to rely on spoken words of cops and witnesses. I get shivers to think about how many wrongly convicted innocent people sat behind bars based on the power of the spoken word.

With technology now, including social media posts, cameras at street traffic lights, surveillance cameras, body cameras, recording devices like smart phones, everyone has a bird's eye view of everyone else. This phenomenon bleeds into the criminal justice system. Now often we can introduce hard evidence depicting the scene in criminal prosecutions, which has completely changed the landscape of evidence presented in the courtrooms.

The public likes to put lawyers in the same vein as the lying witnesses, faulty cops and the imperfect legal system. When they or their little snowflakes get in trouble, perception changes quickly. When someone is wrongly accused of something, or worse yet, their children are, then that same public chases down a good defense lawyer to represent them or their loved ones. Then we are no longer the hated ones but instead the superstars and the magicians.

CHAPTER 42, IN PLAIN SIGHT

A few years ago, eight deputies had to escort me out of court past warring South Orlando Hispanic gang-bangers pointing at me with their index fingers like guns and their thumbs as triggers. My client took a walk on a murder case where he shot a rival gang member in self-defense.

Using Florida's Stand Your Ground law, I showed that my client was justified in using deadly force with his gun because the aggressors had already threatened to kill him and his friend at a party that they were leaving. His friend's teeth had already been knocked out by the attackers while they were in a car in a public parking lot waiting on a third friend and trying to leave.

The law allows citizens to use deadly force with no duty to retreat if they are in a place they have a right to be, they believe such force is necessary to prevent death or great bodily harm or commission of a forcible felony, they did not initiate the aggression, and they are not themselves committing a forcible felony. My client qualified and the court agreed. My client was a free man.

People can get nasty in court with unimaginable threats. A New York phone number has called me all week and hung up as part of the head-trip of the threats against me as the defense attorney. Threats can be scary, but it doesn't deter me from representing the innocent. It has happened before and likely will again. Threats are an occupational hazard.

I actually missed the finger guns. In general, I missed human interactions around the courthouse dramas in 2020. The Orlando courthouse sat virtually empty during most of the Covid crisis. The legal world transitioned into an online attempt at business-as-usual, along with the rest of the world, with Zoom videos in lieu of court appearances. I watched the legal system inner-workings hit another crossroads during my career as technology grasped more control over the courtrooms.

In February 2021, I took part in one of the pilot programs to test bringing back live in-person trials in the haunted hallways on Orange Avenue. After a year of virtual online dealings, I knocked the rust off and suited up for court. I was ready for a bare-knuckle brawl.

On the opposing side, the two young prosecutors continually keyed into their computers for support from their offices in real time over the two-day trial. I don't consider myself a technology person so to watch them tap into records and resources at their fingertips was daunting. They looked like NASA headquarters glued to their laptops. I realized at that very moment, that I may need more online support while in court proceedings to stay competitive.

Against many odds, we won. Old fashioned courtroom know-how and a super confident, almost cocky, client prevailed. The courtroom deputies kept harassing my client during the trial and advised him to move his car from the courthouse parking garage, because he may be getting locked up for a few years. He declined their advice. He was so confident that he would win.

In this courthouse pilot program, my client happened to be an airline pilot. This was another Stand Your Ground case. The pilot was facing Aggravated Assault with a Deadly Weapon, a third-degree felony, and Improper Exhibition of a Dangerous Weapon or Firearm, a first-degree misdemeanor. A few years prior, the pilot was recreationally watching planes fly in and out of an airport where he worked. He was parked in a public parking lot minding his own business. A man who antagonized him repeatedly drove up and harassed him. The pilot protected himself by showing a legal gun. We used the Stand Your Ground law to show how the pilot was legally in the right. If he was found not in the right, he faced up to five years in jail. I previously presented him with a plea deal and he wanted no part of it. He insisted on having his day in court even though a jury trial was a roll of the dice. We were on standby for a trial date and he got his days in court with a mere one-day notice.

At 9:30 p.m. on a Friday night, the pilot and I walked out of the courtroom with a victory. I had walked these halls so many times before, but this time, I felt the success as more satisfying. I realized how much during Covid I had missed being face-to-face with the clients, the jury, the Judges, and the prosecutors. So many details of practicing law had changed since I first started representing clients, but in one year in 2020 procedures shifted dramatically towards technology and away from the human element. I watched in plain sight along with the rest of the world as our whole way of engaging in law and order just switched like a snap of the finger.

Around that same time, I had another humdinger D.U.I. case and I presented the motion in person as the courthouse was starting to open some. It wasn't a particularly special case, but I remember it because with human interaction, lawyering was starting to feel normal to me again. I was on time. The building was eerily empty except an overabundance of security presence. I missed stopping to shoot the shit with the shoeshine guy at the courthouse. Jazz calls me The Cat with Nine Lives or The Phoenix because I've risen from the ashes so many times.

I had on my suits. The business suit I wear for the public. The gold one on the inside I wear for me. I am who I am. I click past the empty shoe-shine chair to the security line with song lyrics from the Everclear song "Like A California King" in my head, "I see you have made yourself a brand new life, Such a cool blue star with a bright new shine, I see you wear your checkered past just like a shining suit of gold ..."

So many people in my everyday life, including clients, have been significant to me. I've had many encouragers and friends. I've had enemies. Then there are the 80 percenters, the ones who like to see people crash and burn. Out of their own insecurities or envy, they like to see a person flop. Even if the rumors or gossip have no truth, 80% of people like to see bad things happen to other people. Some revel in a potentially positive thing going south, like when Weasel-D invented a product and he wasn't successful in his endeavor. That's not right. Maybe there's 20% that are actually caring and compassionate ... maybe 20. I look for those people and keep them in my life if possible.

Despite the onlookers and naysayers and bullies and gossipers, I play to the 20 percenters. I still jump into court on Mondays, with my head held high and an armload of cases that I'm optimistic that I'll win. I still take on the "Vernons" of the world and their legal issues of the day. I still drive to the beach on weekends. I still meet my buddies at the beach to surf or paddleboard, or on my boat to fish, like time never went by since our teen years. I ride my ups and downs with my train wreck of a personal life, but I still manage to find love in my close relationships.

For life, like surfing, the conditions aren't always perfect. Life isn't perfect for anyone. Like the rest of my life, at the end, I'll go out with a bang of some kind. Per usual, it will be a surprise. Until then, each day, I stand up, shake off the obstacles, look for opportunities, and focus on the positives. I do what I do best. I paddle back out.

CHAPTER 43, MEMORIES AT THE MUSEUM

I recently visited the old courthouse where I started my legal career. It's a museum now, The Orange County Regional History Center on East Central Avenue built in 1927. Let that sink in some. My original place of business is now a history museum. Time passes so quickly.

Where I worked in the 1970s to the 1990s looks like an antique store. Thick red velvet drapes frame high windows that were designed to let air circulate before air conditioning was invented. The ornate wallpaper covers walls that are still adorned with large gold-framed portraits of Old-Orlando white men in blue suits. The furnishings are made of a deep mahogany solid wood with leather covered chairs. Gold-gilded chandeliers hang from the high ceiling which was designed acoustically for sound so you wouldn't need microphones or speakers. Behind the judges' bench is a mural depicting the citrus industry with the words, "Equal and Exact Justice to All Men." The 100-year-old building is a metaphor of life in Central Florida as it was. The small, sturdy, richly appointed traditional building still evokes a sense of reverence and community as a gathering place for justice with a human touch.

On the other hand, the new 23-level enormous courthouse on Orange Avenue depicts today's variety of justice which is numbers-based big business. It feels impersonal, loud, gaudy, cheap and made of plastic particle board and flimsy fixtures with bugging devices everywhere. It lacks the warm welcoming sense of the prior building and a past way of life. Orlando calls itself The City Beautiful but it feels more like a concrete hellscape filled with spyware to me. Things change. The community grew dramatically, and with that growth came the need to charge more crimes to more citizens and process the cases quickly and efficiently.

I walked outside to the sprawling plaza past the life-size metal statue of the Florida cracker wrestling an alligator and I paused for another moment. Another meaningful sight lay before me. Frosty's, Swiggs, Casey's and The Stagger Inn beckoned memories of the party nights that went hand in hand with the old courthouse days. The names on East Central Boulevard bar row change, but the vibe is the same. Day drinkers were there slurping down mind-numbing concoctions. The innocent, the guilty, the prosecutors, the defenders, the clerks, the ones who haven't yet encountered the law, and the lucky few who never will, all day drinking together triggered memories. I told a lot of stories, and a lot of stories were told about me on those bar stools.

I arrived in Central Florida in the 1970s, and on this day pondered all that I witnessed during a half century of massive changes in this area.

Things have energy. The historic building has energy. So many memories of Erin the clerk, my lawyer peers, and the judge of my own sentencing came rushing back as I sat quietly for a few moments looking back at the entrance to the old courthouse. I felt melancholy because I waltzed hundreds of clients through that building and I don't remember them. I remember some, but not all. I significantly impacted a lot of people's lives, I hope in a positive way. I feel honored and humbled to have done so.

My daydreaming of my history and of a simpler time was interrupted with the present. My cell phone rang. It was The Boxer. The waves were up and he wanted to surf or paddleboard later that afternoon. Some things change. Some things thankfully do not change.

THE END for now

www.ingramcontent.com/pod-product-compliance
Lightning Source LLC
Chambersburg PA
CBHW070617310726
48982CB00001B/107
9780985526450